The Half-Brothers & Other Stories by Elizabeth Gaskell

Elizabeth Gaskell is equally well known as Mrs Gaskell. When her mother died, she was three months old and she was sent to live in Knutsford, Cheshire with her Aunt Hannah, this setting would become the basis for her novel Cranford. At 22 she married and settled in Manchester to raise her family. Friends with Charlotte Bronte she went on to write her biography and was also highly regarded by a certain Charles Dickens who published her ghost stories in his magazine. Much of her work views the emerging industrial society of Victorian England through her own moral and religious values and has an uncanny ability to look at and report on the many strata of society.

Index of Contents

THE HALF-BROTHERS

My mother was twice married. She never spoke of her first husband, and it is only from other people that I have learnt what little I know about him. I believe she was scarcely seventeen when she was married to him: and he was barely one-and-twenty. He rented a small farm up in Cumberland, somewhere towards the sea-coast; but he was perhaps too young and inexperienced to have the charge of land and cattle: anyhow, his affairs did not prosper, and he fell into ill health, and died of consumption before they had been three years man and wife, leaving my mother a young widow of twenty, with a little child only just able to walk, and the farm on her hands for four years more by the lease, with half the stock on it dead, or sold off one by one to pay the more pressing debts, and with no money to purchase more, or even to buy the provisions needed for the small consumption of every day. There was another child coming, too; and sad and sorry, I believe, she was to think of it. A dreary winter she must have had in her lonesome dwelling, with never another near it for miles around; her sister came to bear her company, and they two planned and plotted how to make every penny they could raise go as far as possible. I can't tell you how it happened that my little sister, whom I never saw, came to sicken and die; but, as if my poor mother's cup was not full enough, only a fortnight before Gregory was born the little girl took ill of scarlet fever, and in a week she lay dead. My mother was, I believe, just stunned with this last blow. My aunt has told me that she did not cry; aunt Fanny would have been thankful if she had; but she sat holding the poor wee lassie's hand and looking in her pretty, pale, dead face, without so much as shedding a tear. And it was all the same, when they had to take her away to be buried. She just kissed the child, and sat her down in the window-seat to watch the little black train of people (neighbours—my aunt, and one far-off cousin, who were all the friends they could muster) go winding away amongst the snow, which had fallen thinly over the country the night before. When my aunt came back from the funeral, she found my mother in the same place, and as dry-eyed as ever. So she continued until after Gregory was born; and, somehow, his coming seemed to loosen the tears, and she cried day and night, till my aunt and the other watcher looked at each other in dismay, and would fain have stopped her if they had but known how. But she bade them let her alone, and not be over-anxious, for every drop she shed eased her brain, which had been in a terrible state before for want of the power to cry. She seemed after that to think of nothing but her new little baby; she had hardly appeared to remember either her husband or her little daughter that lay dead in Brigham churchyard— at least so aunt Fanny said, but she was a great talker, and my mother was very silent by nature, and I think aunt Fanny may have been mistaken in believing that my mother never thought of her husband and child just because she never spoke about them. Aunt Fanny was older than my mother, and had a way of treating her like a child; but, for all that, she was a kind, warm-hearted creature, who thought more of her sister's welfare than she did of her own and it was on her bit of money that they principally lived, and on what the two could earn by working for the great Glasgow sewing-merchants. But by-and-by my mother's eye-sight began to fail. It was not that she was exactly blind, for she could see well enough to guide herself about the house, and to do a good deal of domestic work; but she could no longer do fine sewing and earn money. It must have been with the heavy crying she had had in her day, for she was but a young creature at this time, and as pretty a young woman, I have heard people say, as any on the country side. She took it sadly to heart that she could no longer gain anything towards the keep of herself and her child. My aunt Fanny would fain have persuaded her that she had enough to do in managing their cottage and minding Gregory; but my mother knew that they were pinched, and that aunt Fanny herself had not as much to eat, even of the commonest kind of food, as she could have done with; and as for Gregory, he was not a strong lad, and needed, not more food—for he always had enough, whoever went short—but better nourishment, and more flesh-meat. One day—it was aunt Fanny who told me all this about my poor mother, long after her death—as the sisters were sitting together, aunt Fanny working, and my mother hushing Gregory to sleep, William Preston, who was afterwards my father, came in. He was reckoned an old bachelor; I suppose he was long past forty, and he was one of the wealthiest farmers thereabouts, and had known my grandfather well, and my mother and my aunt in their more prosperous days. He sat down, and began to twirl his hat by way of being agreeable; my aunt Fanny talked, and he listened and looked at my mother. But he said very little, either on that visit, or on many another that he paid before he spoke out what had been the real purpose of his calling so often all along, and from the very first time he came to their house. One Sunday, however, my aunt Fanny stayed away from church, and took care of the child, and my mother went alone. When she came back, she ran straight upstairs, without going into the kitchen to look at Gregory or speak any word to her sister, and aunt Fanny heard her cry as if her heart was breaking; so she went up and scolded her right well through the bolted door, till at last she got her to open it. And then she threw herself on my aunt's neck, and told her that William Preston had asked her to marry him, and had promised to take good charge of her boy, and to let him want for nothing, neither in the way of keep nor of education, and that she had consented. Aunt Fanny was a good deal shocked at this; for, as I have said, she had often thought that my mother had forgotten her first husband very quickly, and now here was proof positive of it, if she could so soon think of marrying again. Besides as aunt Fanny used to say, she herself would have been a far more suitable match for a man of William Preston's age than Helen, who, though she was a widow, had not seen her four-and-twentieth summer. However, as aunt Fanny said, they had not asked her advice; and there was much to be said on the other side of the question. Helen's eyesight would never be good for much again, and as William Preston's wife she would never need to do anything, if she chose to sit with her hands before her; and a boy was a great charge to a widowed mother; and now there would be a decent steady man to see after him. So, by-and-by, aunt Fanny seemed to take a brighter view of the marriage than did my mother herself, who hardly ever looked up, and never smiled after the day when she promised William Preston to be his wife. But much as she had loved Gregory before, she seemed to love him more now. She was continually talking to him when they were alone, though he was far too young to understand her moaning words, or give him any comfort, except by his caresses.

At last William Preston and she were wed; and she went to be mistress of a well-stocked house, not above half-an-hour's walk from where aunt Fanny lived. I believe she did all that she could to please my father; and a more dutiful wife, I have heard him himself say, could never have been. But she did not love him, and he soon found it out. She loved Gregory, and she did not love him. Perhaps, love would have come in time, if he had been patient enough to wait; but it just turned him sour to see how her eye brightened and her colour came at the sight of that little child, while for him who had given her so much, she had only gentle words as cold as ice. He got to taunt her with the difference in her manner, as if that would bring love: and he took a positive dislike to Gregory,—he was so jealous of the ready love that always gushed out like a spring of fresh water when he came near. He wanted her to love him more, and perhaps that was all well and good; but he wanted her to love her child less, and that was an evil wish. One day, he gave way to his temper, and cursed and swore at Gregory, who had got into some mischief, as children will; my mother made some excuse for him; my father said it was hard enough to have to keep another man's child, without having it perpetually held up in its naughtiness by his wife, who ought to be always in the same mind that he was; and so from little they got to more; and the end of it was, that my mother took to her bed before her time, and I was born that very day. My father was glad, and proud, and sorry, all in a breath; glad and proud that a son was born to him; and sorry for his poor wife's state, and to think how his angry words had brought it on. But he was a man who liked better to be angry than sorry, so he soon found out that it was all Gregory's fault, and owed him an additional grudge for having hastened my birth. He had another grudge against him before long. My mother began to sink the day after I was born. My father sent to Carlisle for doctors, and would have coined his heart's blood into gold to save her, if that could have been; but it could not. My aunt Fanny used to say sometimes, that she thought that Helen did not wish to live, and so just let herself die away without trying to take hold on life; but when I questioned her, she owned that my mother did all the doctors bade her do, with the same sort of uncomplaining patience with which she had acted through life. One of her last requests was to have Gregory laid in her bed by my side, and then she made him take hold of my little hand. Her husband came in while she was looking at us so, and when he bent tenderly over her to ask her how she felt now, and seemed to gaze on us two little half-brothers, with a grave sort of kindness, she looked up in his face and smiled, almost her first smile at him; and such a sweet smile! as more besides aunt Fanny have said. In an hour she was dead. Aunt Fanny came to live with us. It was the best thing that could be done. My father would have been glad to return to his old mode of bachelor life, but what could he do with two little children? He needed a woman to take care of him, and who so fitting as his wife's elder sister? So she had the charge of me from my birth; and for a time I was weakly, as was but natural, and she was always beside me, night and day watching over me, and my father nearly as anxious as she. For his land had come down from father to son for more than three hundred years, and he would have cared for me merely as his flesh and blood that was to inherit the land after him. But he needed something to love, for all that, to most people, he was a stern, hard man, and he took to me as, I fancy, he had taken to no human being before—as he might have taken to my mother, if she had had no former life for him to be jealous of. I loved him back again right heartily. I loved all around me, I believe, for everybody was kind to me. After a time, I overcame my original weakness of constitution, and was just a bonny, strong-looking lad whom every passer-by noticed, when my father took me with him to the nearest town.

At home I was the darling of my aunt, the tenderly-beloved of my father, the pet and plaything of the old domestics, the "young master" of the farm-labourers, before whom I played many a lordly antic, assuming a sort of authority which sat oddly enough, I doubt not, on such a baby as I was.

Gregory was three years older than I. Aunt Fanny was always kind to him in deed and in action, but she did not often think about him, she had fallen so completely into the habit of being engrossed by me, from the fact of my having come into her charge as a delicate baby. My father never got over his grudging dislike to his stepson, who had so innocently wrestled with him for the possession of my mother's heart. I mistrust me, too, that my father always considered him as the cause of my mother's death and my early delicacy; and utterly unreasonable as this may seem, I believe my father rather cherished his feeling of alienation to my brother as a duty, than strove to repress it. Yet not for the world would my father have grudged him anything that money could purchase. That was, as it were, in the bond when he had wedded my mother. Gregory was lumpish and loutish, awkward and ungainly, marring whatever he meddled in, and many a hard word and sharp scolding did he get from the people about the farm, who hardly waited till my father's back was turned before they rated the stepson. I am ashamed—my heart is sore to think how I fell into the fashion of the family, and slighted my poor orphan step- brother. I don't think I ever scouted him, or was wilfully ill-natured to him; but the habit of being considered in all things, and being treated as something uncommon and superior, made me insolent in my prosperity, and I exacted more than Gregory was always willing to grant, and then, irritated, I sometimes repeated the disparaging words I had heard others use with regard to him, without fully understanding their meaning. Whether he did or not I cannot tell. I am afraid he did. He used to turn silent and quiet—sullen and sulky, my father thought it: stupid, aunt Fanny used to call it. But every one said he was stupid and dull, and this stupidity and dullness grew upon him. He would sit without speaking a word, sometimes, for hours; then my father would bid him rise and do some piece of work, maybe, about the farm. And he would take three or four tellings before he would go. When we were sent to school, it was all the same. He could never be made to remember his lessons; the school-master grew weary of scolding and flogging, and at last advised my father just to take him away, and set him to some farm- work that might not be above his comprehension. I think he was more gloomy and stupid than ever after this, yet he was not a cross lad; he was patient and good-natured, and would try to do a kind turn for any one, even if they had been scolding or cuffing him not a minute before. But very often his attempts at kindness ended in some mischief to the very people he was trying to serve, owing to his awkward, ungainly ways. I suppose I was a clever lad; at any rate, I always got plenty of praise; and was, as we called it, the cock of the school. The schoolmaster said I could learn anything I chose, but my father, who had no great learning himself, saw little use in much for me, and took me away betimes, and kept me with him about the farm. Gregory was made into a kind of shepherd, receiving his training under old Adam, who was nearly past his work. I think old Adam was almost the first person who had a good opinion of Gregory. He stood to it that my brother had good parts, though he did not rightly know how to bring them out; and, for knowing the bearings of the Fells, he said he had never seen a lad like him. My father would try to bring Adam round to speak of Gregory's faults and shortcomings; but, instead of that, he would praise him twice as much, as soon as he found out what was my father's object.

One winter-time, when I was about sixteen, and Gregory nineteen, I was sent by my father on an errand to a place about seven miles distant by the road, but only about four by the Fells. He bade me return by the road, whichever way I took in going, for the evenings closed in early, and were often thick and misty; besides which, old Adam, now paralytic and bedridden, foretold a downfall of snow before long. I soon got to my journey's end, and soon had done my business; earlier by an hour, I thought, than my father had expected, so I took the decision of the way by which I would return into my own hands, and set off back again over the Fells, just as the first shades of evening began to fall. It looked dark and gloomy enough; but everything was so still that I thought I should have plenty of time to get home before the snow came down. Off I set at a pretty quick pace. But night came on quicker. The right path was clear enough in the day-time, although at several points two or three exactly similar diverged from the same place; but when there was a good light, the traveller was guided by the sight of distant objects,—a piece of rock,—a fall in the ground—which were quite invisible to me now. I plucked up a brave heart, however, and took what seemed to me the right road. It was wrong, nevertheless, and led me whither I knew not, but to some wild boggy moor where the solitude seemed painful, intense, as if never footfall of man had come thither to break the silence. I tried to shout—with the dimmest possible hope of being heard—rather to reassure myself by the sound of my own voice; but my voice came husky and short, and yet it dismayed me; it seemed so weird and strange, in that noiseless expanse of black darkness. Suddenly the air was filled thick with dusky flakes, my face and hands were wet with snow. It cut me off from the slightest knowledge of where I was, for I lost every idea of the direction from which I had come, so that I could not even retrace my steps; it hemmed me in, thicker, thicker, with a darkness that might be felt. The boggy soil on which I stood quaked under me if I remained long in one place, and yet I dared not move far. All my youthful hardiness seemed to leave me at once. I was on the point of crying, and only very shame seemed to keep it down. To save myself from shedding tears, I shouted—terrible, wild shouts for bare life they were. I turned sick as I paused to listen; no answering sound came but the unfeeling echoes. Only the noiseless, pitiless snow kept falling thicker, thicker—faster, faster! I was growing numb and sleepy. I tried to move about, but I dared not go far, for fear of the precipices which, I knew, abounded in certain places on the Fells. Now and then, I stood still and shouted again; but my voice was getting choked with tears, as I thought of the desolate helpless death I was to die, and how little they at home, sitting round the warm, red, bright fire, wotted what was become of me,—and how my poor father would grieve for me—it would surely kill him—it would break his heart, poor old man! Aunt Fanny too—was this to be the end of all her cares for me? I began to review my life in a strange kind of vivid dream, in which the various scenes of my few boyish years passed before me like visions. In a pang of agony, caused by such remembrance of my short life, I gathered up my strength and called out once more, a long, despairing, wailing cry, to which I had no hope of obtaining any answer, save from the echoes around, dulled as the sound might be by the thickened air. To my surprise I heard a cry—almost as long, as wild as mine—so wild that it seemed unearthly, and I almost thought it must be the voice of some of the mocking spirits of the Fells, about whom I had heard so many tales. My heart suddenly began to beat fast and loud. I could not reply for a minute or two. I nearly fancied I had lost the power of utterance. Just at this moment a dog barked. Was it Lassie's bark—my brother's collie?—an ugly enough brute, with a white, ill-looking face, that my father always kicked whenever he saw it, partly for its own demerits, partly because it belonged to my brother. On such occasions, Gregory would whistle Lassie away, and go off and sit with her in some outhouse. My father had once or twice been ashamed of himself, when the poor collie had yowled out with the suddenness of the pain, and had relieved himself of his self-reproach by blaming my brother, who, he said, had no notion of training a dog, and was enough to ruin any collie in Christendom with his stupid way of allowing them to lie by the kitchen fire. To all which Gregory would answer nothing, nor even seem to hear, but go on looking absent and moody.

Yes! there again! It was Lassie's bark! Now or never! I lifted up my voice and shouted "Lassie! Lassie! for God's sake, Lassie!" Another moment, and the great white-faced Lassie was curving and gambolling with delight round my feet and legs, looking, however, up in my face with her intelligent, apprehensive eyes, as if fearing lest I might greet her with a blow, as I had done oftentimes before. But I cried with gladness, as I stooped down and patted her. My mind was sharing in my body's weakness, and I could not reason, but I knew that help was at hand. A gray figure came more and more distinctly out of the thick, close-pressing darkness. It was Gregory wrapped in his maud.

"Oh, Gregory!" said I, and I fell upon his neck, unable to speak another word. He never spoke much, and made me no answer for some little time. Then he told me we must move, we must walk for the dear life—we must find our road home, if possible; but we must move, or we should be frozen to death.

"Don't you know the way home?" asked I.

"I thought I did when I set out, but I am doubtful now. The snow blinds me, and I am feared that in moving about just now, I have lost the right gait homewards."

He had his shepherd's staff with him, and by dint of plunging it before us at every step we took—clinging close to each other, we went on safely enough, as far as not falling down any of the steep rocks, but it was slow, dreary work. My brother, I saw, was more guided by Lassie and the way she took than anything else, trusting to her instinct. It was too dark to see far before us; but he called her back continually, and noted from what quarter she returned, and shaped our slow steps accordingly. But the tedious motion scarcely kept my very blood from freezing. Every bone, every fibre in my body seemed first to ache, and then to swell, and then to turn numb with the intense cold. My brother bore it better than I, from having been more out upon the hills. He did not speak, except to call Lassie. I strove to be brave, and not complain; but now I felt the deadly fatal sleep stealing over me.

"I can go no farther," I said, in a drowsy tone. I remember I suddenly became dogged and resolved. Sleep I would, were it only for five minutes. If death were to be the consequence, sleep I would. Gregory stood still. I suppose, he recognized the peculiar phase of suffering to which I had been brought by the cold.

"It is of no use," said he, as if to himself. "We are no nearer home than we were when we started, as far as I can tell. Our only chance is in Lassie. Here! roll thee in my maud, lad, and lay thee down on this sheltered side of this bit of rock. Creep close under it, lad, and I'll lie by thee, and strive to keep the warmth in us. Stay! hast gotten aught about thee they'll know at home?"

I felt him unkind thus to keep me from slumber, but on his repeating the question, I pulled out my pocket-handkerchief, of some showy pattern, which Aunt Fanny had hemmed for me—Gregory took it, and tied it round Lassie's neck.

"Hie thee, Lassie, hie thee home!" And the white-faced ill-favoured brute was off like a shot in the darkness. Now I might lie down—now I might sleep. In my drowsy stupor I felt that I was being tenderly covered up by my brother; but what with I neither knew nor cared—I was too dull, too selfish, too numb to think and reason, or I might have known that in that bleak bare place there was nought to wrap me in, save what was taken off another. I was glad enough when he ceased his cares and lay down by me. I took his hand.

"Thou canst not remember, lad, how we lay together thus by our dying mother. She put thy small, wee hand in mine—I reckon she sees us now; and belike we shall soon be with her. Anyhow, God's will be done."

"Dear Gregory," I muttered, and crept nearer to him for warmth. He was talking still, and again about our mother, when I fell asleep. In an instant—or so it seemed—there were many voices about me— many faces hovering round me—the sweet luxury of warmth was stealing into every part of me. I was in my own little bed at home. I am thankful to say, my first word was "Gregory?"

A look passed from one to another—my father's stern old face strove in vain to keep its sternness; his mouth quivered, his eyes filled slowly with unwonted tears.

"I would have given him half my land—I would have blessed him as my son,—oh God! I would have knelt at his feet, and asked him to forgive my hardness of heart."

I heard no more. A whirl came through my brain, catching me back to death.

I came slowly to my consciousness, weeks afterwards. My father's hair was white when I recovered, and his hands shook as he looked into my face.

We spoke no more of Gregory. We could not speak of him; but he was strangely in our thoughts. Lassie came and went with never a word of blame; nay, my father would try to stroke her, but she shrank away; and he, as if reproved by the poor dumb beast, would sigh, and be silent and abstracted for a time.

Aunt Fanny—always a talker—told me all. How, on that fatal night, my father,—irritated by my prolonged absence, and probably more anxious than he cared to show, had been fierce and imperious, even beyond his wont, to Gregory; had upbraided him with his father's poverty, his own stupidity which made his services good for nothing—for so, in spite of the old shepherd, my father always chose to consider them. At last, Gregory had risen up, and whistled Lassie out with him—poor Lassie, crouching underneath his chair for fear of a kick or a blow. Some time before, there had been some talk between my father and my aunt respecting my return; and when aunt Fanny told me all this, she said she fancied that Gregory might have noticed the coming storm, and gone out silently to meet me. Three hours afterwards, when all were running about in wild alarm, not knowing whither to go in search of me—not even missing Gregory, or heeding his absence, poor fellow—poor, poor fellow!—Lassie came home, with my handkerchief tied round her neck. They knew and understood, and the whole strength of the farm was turned out to follow her, with wraps, and blankets, and brandy, and every thing that could be thought of. I lay in chilly sleep, but still alive, beneath the rock that Lassie guided them to. I was covered over with my brother's plaid, and his thick shepherd's coat was carefully wrapped round my feet. He was in his shirt-sleeves—his arm thrown over me—a quiet smile (he had hardly ever smiled in life) upon his still, cold face.

My father's last words were, "God forgive me my hardness of heart towards the fatherless child!"

And what marked the depth of his feeling of repentance, perhaps more than all, considering the passionate love he bore my mother, was this: we found a paper of directions after his death, in which he desired that he might lie at the foot of the grave, in which, by his desire, poor Gregory had been laid with OUR MOTHER.

HALF A LIFE-TIME AGO

CHAPTER I

HALF a life-time ago, there lived in one of the Westmoreland dales a single woman, of the name of Susan Dixon. She was owner of the small farm-house where she resided, and of some thirty or forty acres of land by which it was surrounded. She had also an hereditary right to a sheep-walk, extending to the wild fells that overhang Blea Tarn. In the language of the country she was a Stateswoman. Her house is yet to be seen on the Oxenfell road, between Skelwith and Coniston. You go along a moorland track, made by the carts that occasionally came for turf from the Oxenfell. A brook babbles and brattles by the wayside, giving you a sense of companionship, which relieves the deep solitude in which this way is usually traversed. Some miles on this side of Coniston there is a farmstead—a gray stone house, and a square of farm-buildings surrounding a green space of rough turf, in the midst of which stands a mighty, funereal umbrageous yew, making a solemn shadow, as of death, in the very heart and centre of the light and heat of the brightest summer day. On the side away from the house, this yard slopes down to a dark-brown pool, which is supplied with fresh water from the overflowings of a stone cistern, into which some rivulet of the brook before-mentioned continually and melodiously falls bubbling. The cattle drink out of this cistern. The household bring their pitchers and fill them with drinking-water by a dilatory, yet pretty, process. The water-carrier brings with her a leaf of the hound's-tongue fern, and, inserting it in the crevice of the gray rock, makes a cool, green spout for the sparkling stream.

The house is no specimen, at the present day, of what it was in the lifetime of Susan Dixon. Then, every small diamond pane in the windows glittered with cleanliness. You might have eaten off the floor; you could see yourself in the pewter plates and the polished oaken awmry, or dresser, of the state kitchen into which you entered. Few strangers penetrated further than this room. Once or twice, wandering tourists, attracted by the lonely picturesqueness of the situation, and the exquisite cleanliness of the house itself, made their way into this house-place, and offered money enough (as they thought) to tempt the hostess to receive them as lodgers. They would give no trouble, they said; they would be out rambling or sketching all day long; would be perfectly content with a share of the food which she provided for herself; or would procure what they required from the Waterhead Inn at Coniston. But no liberal sum—no fair words—moved her from her stony manner, or her monotonous tone of indifferent refusal. No persuasion could induce her to show any more of the house than that first room; no appearance of fatigue procured for the weary an invitation to sit down and rest; and if one more bold and less delicate did so without being asked, Susan stood by, cold and apparently deaf, or only replying by the briefest monosyllables, till the unwelcome visitor had departed. Yet those with whom she had dealings, in the way of selling her cattle or her farm produce, spoke of her as keen after a bargain—a hard one to have to do with; and she never spared herself exertion or fatigue, at market or in the field, to make the most of her produce. She led the hay-makers with her swift, steady rake, and her noiseless evenness of motion. She was about among the earliest in the market, examining samples of oats, pricing them, and then turning with grim satisfaction to her own cleaner corn.

She was served faithfully and long by those who were rather her fellow-labourers than her servants. She was even and just in her dealings with them. If she was peculiar and silent, they knew her, and knew that she might be relied on. Some of them had known her from her childhood; and deep in their hearts was an unspoken—almost unconscious—pity for her, for they knew her story, though they never spoke of it.

Yes; the time had been when that tall, gaunt, hard-featured, angular woman—who never smiled, and hardly ever spoke an unnecessary word—had been a fine-looking girl, bright-spirited and rosy; and when the hearth at the Yew Nook had been as bright as she, with family love and youthful hope and mirth. Fifty or fifty-one years ago, William Dixon and his wife Margaret were alive; and Susan, their daughter, was about eighteen years old—ten years older than the only other child, a boy named after his father. William and Margaret Dixon were rather superior people, of a character belonging—as far as I have seen—exclusively to the class of Westmoreland and Cumberland statesmen—just, independent, upright; not given to much speaking; kind-hearted, but not demonstrative; disliking change, and new ways, and new people; sensible and shrewd; each household self-contained, and its members having little curiosity as to their neighbours, with whom they rarely met for any social intercourse, save at the stated times of sheep-shearing and Christmas; having a certain kind of sober pleasure in amassing money, which occasionally made them miserable (as they call miserly people up in the north) in their old age; reading no light or ephemeral literature, but the grave, solid books brought round by the pedlars (such as the "Paradise Lost" and "Regained,'" "The Death of Abel," "The Spiritual Quixote," and "The Pilgrim's Progress"), were to be found in nearly every house: the men occasionally going off laking, i.e. playing, i.e. drinking for days together, and having to be hunted up by anxious wives, who dared not leave their husbands to the chances of the wild precipitous roads, but walked miles and miles, lantern in hand, in the dead of night, to discover and guide the solemnly-drunken husband home; who had a dreadful headache the next day, and the day after that came forth as grave, and sober, and virtuous looking as if there were no such thing as malt and spirituous liquors in the world; and who were seldom reminded of their misdoings by their wives, to whom such occasional outbreaks were as things of course, when once the immediate anxiety produced by them was over. Such were—such are—the characteristics of a class now passing away from the face of the land, as their compeers, the yeomen, have done before them. Of such was William Dixon. He was a shrewd clever farmer, in his day and generation, when shrewdness was rather shown in the breeding and rearing of sheep and cattle than in the cultivation of land. Owing to this character of his, statesmen from a distance from beyond Kendal, or from Borrowdale, of greater wealth than he, would send their sons to be farm-servants for a year or two with him, in order to learn some of his methods before setting up on land of their own. When Susan, his daughter, was about seventeen, one Michael Hurst was farm-servant at Yew Nook. He worked with the master, and lived with the family, and was in all respects treated as an equal, except in the field. His father was a wealthy statesman at Wythburne, up beyond Grasmere; and through Michael's servitude the families had become acquainted, and the Dixons went over to the High Beck sheep-shearing, and the Hursts came down by Red Bank and Loughrig Tarn and across the Oxenfell when there was the Christmas-tide feasting at Yew Nook. The fathers strolled round the fields together, examined cattle and sheep, and looked knowing over each other's horses. The mothers inspected the dairies and household arrangements, each openly admiring the plans of the other, but secretly preferring their own. Both fathers and mothers cast a glance from time to time at Michael and Susan, who were thinking of nothing less than farm or dairy, but whose unspoken attachment was, in all ways, so suitable and natural a thing that each parent rejoiced over it, although with characteristic reserve it was never spoken about—not even between husband and wife.

Susan had been a strong, independent, healthy girl; a clever help to her mother, and a spirited companion to her father; more of a man in her (as he often said) than her delicate little brother ever would have. He was his mother's darling, although she loved Susan well. There was no positive engagement between Michael and Susan—I doubt whether even plain words of love had been spoken; when one winter-time Margaret Dixon was seized with inflammation consequent upon a neglected cold. She had always been strong and notable, and had been too busy to attend to the early symptoms of illness. It would go off, she said to the woman who helped in the kitchen; or if she did not feel better when they had got the hams and bacon out of hand, she would take some herb-tea and nurse up a bit. But Death could not wait till the hams and bacon were cured: he came on with rapid strides, and shooting arrows of portentous agony. Susan had never seen illness—never knew how much she loved her mother till now, when she felt a dreadful, instinctive certainty that she was losing her. Her mind was thronged with recollections of the many times she had slighted her mother's wishes; her heart was full of the echoes of careless and angry replies that she had spoken. What would she not now give to have opportunities of service and obedience, and trials of her patience and love, for that dear mother who lay gasping in torture! And yet Susan had been a good girl and an affectionate daughter.

The sharp pain went off, and delicious ease came on; yet still her mother sunk. In the midst of this languid peace she was dying. She motioned Susan to her bedside, for she could only whisper; and then, while the father was out of the room, she spoke as much to the eager, hungering eyes of her daughter by the motion of her lips, as by the slow, feeble sounds of her voice.

"Susan, lass, thou must not fret. It is God's will, and thou wilt have a deal to do. Keep father straight if thou canst; and if he goes out Ulverstone ways, see that thou meet him before he gets to the Old Quarry. It's a dree bit for a man who has had a drop. As for lile Will"—Here the poor woman's face began to work and her fingers to move nervously as they lay on the bed-quilt—"lile Will will miss me most of all. Father's often vexed with him because he's not a quick strong lad; he is not, my poor lile chap. And father thinks he's saucy, because he cannot always stomach oat-cake and porridge. There's better than three pound in th' old black tea-pot on the top shelf of the cupboard. Just keep a piece of loaf-bread by you, Susan dear, for Will to come to when he's not taken his breakfast. I have, may be, spoilt him; but there'll be no one to spoil him now."

She began to cry a low, feeble cry, and covered up her face that Susan might not see her. That dear face! those precious moments while yet the eyes could look out with love and intelligence. Susan laid her head down close by her mother's ear.

"Mother I'll take tent of Will. Mother, do you hear? He shall not want ought I can give or get for him, least of all the kind words which you had ever ready for us both. Bless you! bless you! my own mother."

"Thou'lt promise me that, Susan, wilt thou? I can die easy if thou'lt take charge of him. But he's hardly like other folk; he tries father at times, though I think father'll be tender of him when I'm gone, for my sake. And, Susan, there's one thing more. I never spoke on it for fear of the bairn being called a tell-tale, but I just comforted him up. He vexes Michael at times, and Michael has struck him before now. I did not want to make a stir; but he's not strong, and a word from thee, Susan, will go a long way with Michael."

Susan was as red now as she had been pale before; it was the first time that her influence over Michael had been openly acknowledged by a third person, and a flash of joy came athwart the solemn sadness of the moment. Her mother had spoken too much, and now came on the miserable faintness. She never spoke again coherently; but when her children and her husband stood by her bedside, she took lile Will's hand and put it into Susan's, and looked at her with imploring eyes. Susan clasped her arms round Will, and leaned her head upon his little curly one, and vowed within herself to be as a mother to him.

Henceforward she was all in all to her brother. She was a more spirited and amusing companion to him than his mother had been, from her greater activity, and perhaps, also, from her originality of character, which often prompted her to perform her habitual actions in some new and racy manner. She was tender to lile Will when she was prompt and sharp with everybody else—with Michael most of all; for somehow the girl felt that, unprotected by her mother, she must keep up her own dignity, and not allow her lover to see how strong a hold he had upon her heart. He called her hard and cruel, and left her so; and she smiled softly to herself, when his back was turned, to think how little he guessed how deeply he was loved. For Susan was merely comely and fine looking; Michael was strikingly handsome, admired by all the girls for miles round, and quite enough of a country coxcomb to know it and plume himself accordingly. He was the second son of his father; the eldest would have High Beck farm, of course, but there was a good penny in the Kendal bank in store for Michael. When harvest was over, he went to Chapel Langdale to learn to dance; and at night, in his merry moods, he would do his steps on the flag floor of the Yew Nook kitchen, to the secret admiration of Susan, who had never learned dancing, but who flouted him perpetually, even while she admired, in accordance with the rule she seemed to have made for herself about keeping him at a distance so long as he lived under the same roof with her. One evening he sulked at some saucy remark of hers; he sitting in the chimney corner with his arms on his knees, and his head bent forwards, lazily gazing into the wood-fire on the hearth, and luxuriating in rest after a hard day's labour; she sitting among the geraniums on the long, low window-seat, trying to catch the last slanting rays of the autumnal light to enable her to finish stitching a shirt-collar for Will, who lounged full length on the flags at the other side of the hearth to Michael, poking the burning wood from time to time with a long hazel-stick to bring out the leap of glittering sparks.

"And if you can dance a threesome reel, what good does it do ye?" asked Susan, looking askance at Michael, who had just been vaunting his proficiency. "Does it help you plough, reap, or even climb the rocks to take a raven's nest? If I were a man, I'd be ashamed to give in to such softness."

"If you were a man, you'd be glad to do anything which made the pretty girls stand round and admire."

"As they do to you, eh! Ho, Michael, that would not be my way o' being a man!"

"What would then?" asked he, after a pause, during which he had expected in vain that she would go on with her sentence. No answer.

"I should not like you as a man, Susy; you'd be too hard and headstrong."

"Am I hard and headstrong?" asked she, with as indifferent a tone as she could assume, but which yet had a touch of pique in it. His quick ear detected the inflexion.

"No, Susy! You're wilful at times, and that's right enough. I don't like a girl without spirit. There's a mighty pretty girl comes to the dancing class; but she is all milk and water. Her eyes never flash like yours when you're put out; why, I can see them flame across the kitchen like a cat's in the dark. Now, if you were a man, I should feel queer before those looks of yours; as it is, I rather like them, because—"

"Because what?" asked she, looking up and perceiving that he had stolen close up to her.

"Because I can make all right in this way," said he, kissing her suddenly.

"Can you?" said she, wrenching herself out of his grasp and panting, half with rage. "Take that, by way of proof that making right is none so easy." And she boxed his ears pretty sharply. He went back to his seat discomfited and out of temper. She could no longer see to look, even if her face had not burnt and her eyes dazzled, but she did not choose to move her seat, so she still preserved her stooping attitude and pretended to go on sewing.

"Eleanor Hebthwaite may be milk-and-water," muttered he, "but—Confound thee, lad! what art thou doing?" exclaimed Michael, as a great piece of burning wood was cast into his face by an unlucky poke of Will's. "Thou great lounging, clumsy chap, I'll teach thee better!" and with one or two good round kicks he sent the lad whimpering away into the back-kitchen. When he had a little recovered himself from his passion, he saw Susan standing before him, her face looking strange and almost ghastly by the reversed position of the shadows, arising from the firelight shining upwards right under it.

"I tell thee what, Michael," said she, "that lad's motherless, but not friendless."

"His own father leathers him, and why should not I, when he's given me such a burn on my face?" said Michael, putting up his hand to his cheek as if in pain.

"His father's his father, and there is nought more to be said. But if he did burn thee, it was by accident, and not o' purpose; as thou kicked him, it's a mercy if his ribs are not broken."

"He howls loud enough, I'm sure. I might ha' kicked many a lad twice as hard, and they'd ne'er ha' said ought but 'damn ye;' but yon lad must needs cry out like a stuck pig if one touches him;" replied Michael, sullenly.

Susan went back to the window-seat, and looked absently out of the window at the drifting clouds for a minute or two, while her eyes filled with tears. Then she got up and made for the outer door which led into the back-kitchen. Before she reached it, however, she heard a low voice, whose music made her thrill, say—

"Susan, Susan!"

Her heart melted within her, but it seemed like treachery to her poor boy, like faithlessness to her dead mother, to turn to her lover while the tears which he had caused to flow were yet unwiped on Will's cheeks. So she seemed to take no heed, but passed into the darkness, and, guided by the sobs, she found her way to where Willie sat crouched among the disused tubs and churns.

"Come out wi' me, lad;" and they went out into the orchard, where the fruit-trees were bare of leaves, but ghastly in their tattered covering of gray moss: and the soughing November wind came with long sweeps over the fells till it rattled among the crackling boughs, underneath which the brother and sister sat in the dark; he in her lap, and she hushing his head against her shoulder.

"Thou should'st na' play wi' fire. It's a naughty trick. Thou't suffer for it in worse ways nor this before thou'st done, I'm afeared. I should ha' hit thee twice as lungeous kicks as Mike, if I'd been in his place. He did na' hurt thee, I am sure," she assumed, half as a question.

"Yes but he did. He turned me quite sick." And he let his head fall languidly down on his sister's breast.

"Come, lad! come, lad!" said she anxiously. "Be a man. It was not much that I saw. Why, when first the red cow came she kicked me far harder for offering to milk her before her legs were tied. See thee! here's a peppermint-drop, and I'll make thee a pasty to-night; only don't give way so, for it hurts me sore to think that Michael has done thee any harm, my pretty."

Willie roused himself up, and put back the wet and ruffled hair from his heated face; and he and Susan rose up, and hand-in-hand went towards the house, walking slowly and quietly except for a kind of sob which Willie could not repress. Susan took him to the pump and washed his tear-stained face, till she thought she had obliterated all traces of the recent disturbance, arranging his curls for him, and then she kissed him tenderly, and led him in, hoping to find Michael in the kitchen, and make all straight between them. But the blaze had dropped down into darkness; the wood was a heap of gray ashes in which the sparks ran hither and thither; but even in the groping darkness Susan knew by the sinking at her heart that Michael was not there. She threw another brand on the hearth and lighted the candle, and sat down to her work in silence. Willie cowered on his stool by the side of the fire, eyeing his sister from time to time, and sorry and oppressed, he knew not why, by the sight of her grave, almost stern face. No one came. They two were in the house alone. The old woman who helped Susan with the household work had gone out for the night to some friend's dwelling. William Dixon, the father, was up on the fells seeing after his sheep. Susan had no heart to prepare the evening meal.

"Susy, darling, are you angry with me?" said Willie, in his little piping, gentle voice. He had stolen up to his sister's side. "I won't never play with the fire again; and I'll not cry if Michael does kick me. Only don't look so like dead mother—don't—don't—please don't!" he exclaimed, hiding his face on her shoulder.

"I'm not angry, Willie," said she. "Don't be feared on me. You want your supper, and you shall have it; and don't you be feared on Michael. He shall give reason for every hair of your head that he touches— he shall."

When William Dixon came home he found Susan and Willie sitting together, hand-in-hand, and apparently pretty cheerful. He bade them go to bed, for that he would sit up for Michael; and the next morning, when Susan came down, she found that Michael had started an hour before with the cart for lime. It was a long day's work; Susan knew it would be late, perhaps later than on the preceding night, before he returned—at any rate, past her usual bed-time; and on no account would she stop up a minute beyond that hour in the kitchen, whatever she might do in her bed-room. Here she sat and watched till past midnight; and when she saw him coming up the brow with the carts, she knew full well, even in that faint moonlight, that his gait was the gait of a man in liquor. But though she was annoyed and mortified to find in what way he had chosen to forget her, the fact did not disgust or shock her as it would have done many a girl, even at that day, who had not been brought up as Susan had, among a class who considered it no crime, but rather a mark of spirit, in a man to get drunk occasionally. Nevertheless, she chose to hold herself very high all the next day when Michael was, perforce, obliged to give up any attempt to do heavy work, and hung about the out-buildings and farm in a very disconsolate and sickly state. Willie had far more pity on him than Susan. Before evening, Willie and he were fast, and, on his side, ostentatious friends. Willie rode the horses down to water; Willie helped him to chop wood. Susan sat gloomily at her work, hearing an indistinct but cheerful conversation going on in the shippon, while the cows were being milked. She almost felt irritated with her little brother, as if he were a traitor, and had gone over to the enemy in the very battle that she was fighting in his cause. She was alone with no one to speak to, while they prattled on regardless if she were glad or sorry.

Soon Willie burst in. "Susan! Susan! come with me; I've something so pretty to show you. Round the corner of the barn—run! run!" (He was dragging her along, half reluctant, half desirous of some change in that weary day.) Round the corner of the barn; and caught hold of by Michael, who stood there awaiting her.

"O Willie!" cried she "you naughty boy. There is nothing pretty—what have you brought me here for? Let me go; I won't be held."

"Only one word. Nay, if you wish it so much, you may go," said Michael, suddenly loosing his hold as she struggled. But now she was free, she only drew off a step or two, murmuring something about Willie.

"You are going, then?" said Michael, with seeming sadness. "You won't hear me say a word of what is in my heart."

"How can I tell whether it is what I should like to hear?" replied she, still drawing back.

"That is just what I want you to tell me; I want you to hear it and then to tell me whether you like it or not."

"Well, you may speak," replied she, turning her back, and beginning to plait the hem of her apron.

He came close to her ear.

"I'm sorry I hurt Willie the other night. He has forgiven me. Can you?"

"You hurt him very badly," she replied. "But you are right to be sorry. I forgive you."

"Stop, stop!" said he, laying his hand upon her arm. "There is something more I've got to say. I want you to be my—what is it they call it, Susan?"

"I don't know," said she, half-laughing, but trying to get away with all her might now; and she was a strong girl, but she could not manage it.

"You do. My—what is it I want you to be?"

"I tell you I don't know, and you had best be quiet, and just let me go in, or I shall think you're as bad now as you were last night."

"And how did you know what I was last night? It was past twelve when I came home. Were you watching? Ah, Susan! be my wife, and you shall never have to watch for a drunken husband. If I were your husband, I would come straight home, and count every minute an hour till I saw your bonny face. Now you know what I want you to be. I ask you to be my wife. Will you, my own dear Susan?"

She did not speak for some time. Then she only said "Ask father." And now she was really off like a lapwing round the corner of the barn, and up in her own little room, crying with all her might, before the triumphant smile had left Michael's face where he stood.

The "Ask father" was a mere form to be gone though. Old Daniel Hurst and William Dixon had talked over what they could respectively give their children before this; and that was the parental way of arranging such matters. When the probable amount of worldly gear that he could give his child had been named by each father, the young folk, as they said, might take their own time in coming to the point which the old men, with the prescience of experience, saw they were drifting to; no need to hurry them, for they were both young, and Michael, though active enough, was too thoughtless, old Daniel said, to be trusted with the entire management of a farm. Meanwhile, his father would look about him, and see after all the farms that were to be let.

Michael had a shrewd notion of this preliminary understanding between the fathers, and so felt less daunted than he might otherwise have done at making the application for Susan's hand. It was all right, there was not an obstacle; only a deal of good advice, which the lover thought might have as well been spared, and which it must be confessed he did not much attend to, although he assented to every part of it. Then Susan was called down stairs, and slowly came dropping into view down the steps which led from the two family apartments into the house-place. She tried to look composed and quiet, but it could not be done. She stood side by side with her lover, with her head drooping, her cheeks burning, not daring to look up or move, while her father made the newly-betrothed a somewhat formal address in which he gave his consent, and many a piece of worldly wisdom beside. Susan listened as well as she could for the beating of her heart; but when her father solemnly and sadly referred to his own lost wife, she could keep from sobbing no longer; but throwing her apron over her face, she sat down on the bench by the dresser, and fairly gave way to pent-up tears. Oh, how strangely sweet to be comforted as she was comforted, by tender caress, and many a low-whispered promise of love! Her father sat by the fire, thinking of the days that were gone; Willie was still out of doors; but Susan and Michael felt no one's presence or absence—they only knew they were together as betrothed husband and wife.

In a week, or two, they were formally told of the arrangements to be made in their favour. A small farm in the neighbourhood happened to fall vacant; and Michael's father offered to take it for him, and be responsible for the rent for the first year, while William Dixon was to contribute a certain amount of stock, and both fathers were to help towards the furnishing of the house. Susan received all this information in a quiet, indifferent way; she did not care much for any of these preparations, which were to hurry her through the happy hours; she cared least of all for the money amount of dowry and of substance. It jarred on her to be made the confidante of occasional slight repinings of Michael's, as one by one his future father-in-law set aside a beast or a pig for Susan's portion, which were not always the best animals of their kind upon the farm. But he also complained of his own father's stinginess, which somewhat, though not much, alleviated Susan's dislike to being awakened out of her pure dream of love to the consideration of worldly wealth.

But in the midst of all this bustle, Willie moped and pined. He had the same chord of delicacy running through his mind that made his body feeble and weak. He kept out of the way, and was apparently occupied in whittling and carving uncouth heads on hazel-sticks in an out-house. But he positively avoided Michael, and shrunk away even from Susan. She was too much occupied to notice this at first. Michael pointed it out to her, saying, with a laugh,—

"Look at Willie! he might be a cast-off lover and jealous of me, he looks so dark and downcast at me." Michael spoke this jest out loud, and Willie burst into tears, and ran out of the house.

"Let me go. Let me go!" said Susan (for her lover's arm was round her waist). "I must go to him if he's fretting. I promised mother I would!" She pulled herself away, and went in search of the boy. She sought in byre and barn, through the orchard, where indeed in this leafless winter-time there was no great concealment; up into the room where the wool was usually stored in the later summer, and at last she found him, sitting at bay, like some hunted creature, up behind the wood-stack.

"What are ye gone for, lad, and me seeking you everywhere?" asked she, breathless.

"I did not know you would seek me. I've been away many a time, and no one has cared to seek me," said he, crying afresh.

"Nonsense," replied Susan, "don't be so foolish, ye little good-for-nought." But she crept up to him in the hole he had made underneath the great, brown sheafs of wood, and squeezed herself down by him. "What for should folk seek after you, when you get away from them whenever you can?" asked she.

"They don't want me to stay. Nobody wants me. If I go with father, he says I hinder more than I help. You used to like to have me with you. But now, you've taken up with Michael, and you'd rather I was away; and I can just bide away; but I cannot stand Michael jeering at me. He's got you to love him and that might serve him."

"But I love you, too, dearly, lad!" said she, putting her arm round his neck.

"Which on us do you like best?" said he, wistfully, after a little pause, putting her arm away, so that he might look in her face, and see if she spoke truth.

She went very red.

"You should not ask such questions. They are not fit for you to ask, nor for me to answer."

"But mother bade you love me!" said he, plaintively.

"And so I do. And so I ever will do. Lover nor husband shall come betwixt thee and me, lad—ne'er a one of them. That I promise thee (as I promised mother before), in the sight of God and with her hearkening now, if ever she can hearken to earthly word again. Only I cannot abide to have thee fretting, just because my heart is large enough for two."

"And thou'lt love me always?"

"Always, and ever. And the more—the more thou'lt love Michael," said she, dropping her voice.

"I'll try," said the boy, sighing, for he remembered many a harsh word and blow of which his sister knew nothing. She would have risen up to go away, but he held her tight, for here and now she was all his own, and he did not know when such a time might come again. So the two sat crouched up and silent, till they heard the horn blowing at the field-gate, which was the summons home to any wanderers belonging to the farm, and at this hour of the evening, signified that supper was ready. Then the two went in.

CHAPTER II

SUSAN and Michael were to be married in April. He had already gone to take possession of his new farm, three or four miles away from Yew Nook—but that is neighbouring, according to the acceptation of the word in that thinly-populated district,—when William Dixon fell ill. He came home one evening, complaining of head-ache and pains in his limbs, but seemed to loathe the posset which Susan prepared for him; the treacle-posset which was the homely country remedy against an incipient cold. He took to his bed with a sensation of exceeding weariness, and an odd, unusual looking-back to the days of his youth, when he was a lad living with his parents, in this very house.

The next morning he had forgotten all his life since then, and did not know his own children; crying, like a newly-weaned baby, for his mother to come and soothe away his terrible pain. The doctor from Coniston said it was the typhus-fever, and warned Susan of its infectious character, and shook his head over his patient. There were no near friends to come and share her anxiety; only good, kind old Peggy, who was faithfulness itself, and one or two labourers' wives, who would fain have helped her, had not their hands been tied by their responsibility to their own families. But, somehow, Susan neither feared nor flagged. As for fear, indeed, she had no time to give way to it, for every energy of both body and mind was required. Besides, the young have had too little experience of the danger of infection to dread it much. She did indeed wish, from time to time, that Michael had been at home to have taken Willie over to his father's at High Beck; but then, again, the lad was docile and useful to her, and his fecklessness in many things might make him harshly treated by strangers; so, perhaps, it was as well that Michael was away at Appleby fair, or even beyond that—gone into Yorkshire after horses.

Her father grew worse; and the doctor insisted on sending over a nurse from Coniston. Not a professed nurse—Coniston could not have supported such a one; but a widow who was ready to go where the doctor sent her for the sake of the payment. When she came, Susan suddenly gave way; she was felled by the fever herself, and lay unconscious for long weeks. Her consciousness returned to her one spring afternoon; early spring: April,—her wedding-month. There was a little fire burning in the small corner-grate, and the flickering of the blaze was enough for her to notice in her weak state. She felt that there was some one sitting on the window-side of her bed, behind the curtain, but she did not care to know who it was; it was even too great a trouble for her languid mind to consider who it was likely to be. She would rather shut her eyes, and melt off again into the gentle luxury of sleep. The next time she wakened, the Coniston nurse perceived her movement, and made her a cup of tea, which she drank with eager relish; but still they did not speak, and once more Susan lay motionless—not asleep, but strangely, pleasantly conscious of all the small chamber and household sounds; the fall of a cinder on the hearth, the fitful singing of the half-empty kettle, the cattle tramping out to field again after they had been milked, the aged step on the creaking stair—old Peggy's, as she knew. It came to her door; it stopped; the person outside listened for a moment, and then lifted the wooden latch, and looked in. The watcher by the bedside arose, and went to her. Susan would have been glad to see Peggy's face once more, but was far too weak to turn, so she lay and listened.

"How is she?" whispered one trembling, aged voice.

"Better," replied the other. "She's been awake, and had a cup of tea. She'll do now."

"Has she asked after him?"

"Hush! No; she has not spoken a word."

"Poor lass! poor lass!"

The door was shut. A weak feeling of sorrow and self-pity came over Susan. What was wrong? Whom had she loved? And dawning, dawning, slowly rose the sun of her former life, and all particulars were made distinct to her. She felt that some sorrow was coming to her, and cried over it before she knew what it was, or had strength enough to ask. In the dead of night,—and she had never slept again,—she softly called to the watcher, and asked—

"Who?"

"Who what?" replied the woman, with a conscious affright, ill-veiled by a poor assumption of ease. "Lie still, there's a darling, and go to sleep. Sleep's better for you than all the doctor's stuff."

"Who?" repeated Susan. "Something is wrong. Who?"

"Oh, dear!" said the woman. "There's nothing wrong. Willie has taken the turn, and is doing nicely."

"Father?"

"Well! he's all right now," she answered, looking another way, as if seeking for something.

"Then it's Michael! Oh, me! oh, me!" She set up a succession of weak, plaintive, hysterical cries before the nurse could pacify her, by declaring that Michael had been at the house not three hours before to ask after her, and looked as well and as hearty as ever man did.

"And you heard of no harm to him since?" inquired Susan.

"Bless the lass, no, for sure! I've ne'er heard his name named since I saw him go out of the yard as stout a man as ever trod shoe-leather."

It was well, as the nurse said afterwards to Peggy, that Susan had been so easily pacified by the equivocating answer in respect to her father. If she had pressed the questions home in his case as she did in Michael's, she would have learnt that he was dead and buried more than a month before. It was well, too, that in her weak state of convalescence (which lasted long after this first day of consciousness) her perceptions were not sharp enough to observe the sad change that had taken place in Willie. His bodily strength returned, his appetite was something enormous, but his eyes wandered continually; his regard could not be arrested; his speech became slow, impeded, and incoherent. People began to say that the fever had taken away the little wit Willie Dixon had ever possessed and that they feared that he would end in being a "natural," as they call an idiot in the Dales.

The habitual affection and obedience to Susan lasted longer than any other feeling that the boy had had previous to his illness; and, perhaps, this made her be the last to perceive what every one else had long anticipated. She felt the awakening rude when it did come. It was in this wise:—

One Jane evening, she sat out of doors under the yew-tree, knitting. She was pale still from her recent illness; and her languor, joined to the fact of her black dress, made her look more than usually interesting. She was no longer the buoyant self-sufficient Susan, equal to every occasion. The men were bringing in the cows to be milked, and Michael was about in the yard giving orders and directions with somewhat the air of a master, for the farm belonged of right to Willie, and Susan had succeeded to the guardianship of her brother. Michael and she were to be married as soon as she was strong enough— so, perhaps, his authoritative manner was justified; but the labourers did not like it, although they said little. They remembered a stripling on the farm, knowing far less than they did, and often glad to shelter his ignorance of all agricultural matters behind their superior knowledge. They would have taken orders from Susan with far more willingness; nay, Willie himself might have commanded them; and from the old hereditary feeling toward the owners of land, they would have obeyed him with far greater cordiality than they now showed to Michael. But Susan was tired with even three rounds of knitting, and seemed not to notice, or to care, how things went on around her; and Willie—poor Willie!—there he stood lounging against the door-sill, enormously grown and developed, to be sure, but with restless eyes and ever-open mouth, and every now and then setting up a strange kind of howling cry, and then smiling vacantly to himself at the sound he had made. As the two old labourers passed him, they looked at each other ominously, and shook their heads.

"Willie, darling," said Susan, "don't make that noise—it makes my head ache."

She spoke feebly, and Willie did not seem to hear; at any rate, he continued his howl from time to time.

"Hold thy noise, wilt'a?" said Michael, roughly, as he passed near him, and threatening him with his fist. Susan's back was turned to the pair. The expression of Willie's face changed from vacancy to fear, and he came shambling up to Susan, who put her arm round him, and, as if protected by that shelter, he began making faces at Michael. Susan saw what was going on, and, as if now first struck by the strangeness of her brother's manner, she looked anxiously at Michael for an explanation. Michael was irritated at Willie's defiance of him, and did not mince the matter.

"It's just that the fever has left him silly—he never was as wise as other folk, and now I doubt if he will ever get right."

Susan did not speak, but she went very pale, and her lip quivered. She looked long and wistfully at Willie's face, as he watched the motion of the ducks in the great stable-pool. He laughed softly to himself every now and then.

"Willie likes to see the ducks go overhead," said Susan, instinctively adopting the form of speech she would have used to a young child.

"Willie, boo! Willie, boo!" he replied, clapping his hands, and avoiding her eye.

"Speak properly, Willie," said Susan, making a strong effort at self-control, and trying to arrest his attention.

"You know who I am—tell me my name!" She grasped his arm almost painfully tight to make him attend. Now he looked at her, and, for an instant, a gleam of recognition quivered over his face; but the exertion was evidently painful, and he began to cry at the vainness of the effort to recall her name. He hid his face upon her shoulder with the old affectionate trick of manner. She put him gently away, and went into the house into her own little bedroom. She locked the door, and did not reply at all to Michael's calls for her, hardly spoke to old Peggy, who tried to tempt her out to receive some homely sympathy, and through the open easement there still came the idiotic sound of "Willie, boo! Willie, boo!"

CHAPTER III

AFTER the stun of the blow came the realization of the consequences. Susan would sit for hours trying patiently to recall and piece together fragments of recollection and consciousness in her brother's mind. She would let him go and pursue some senseless bit of play, and wait until she could catch his eye or his attention again, when she would resume her self-imposed task. Michael complained that she never had a word for him, or a minute of time to spend with him now; but she only said she must try, while there was yet a chance, to bring back her brother's lost wits. As for marriage in this state of uncertainty, she had no heart to think of it. Then Michael stormed, and absented himself for two or three days; but it was of no use. When he came back, he saw that she had been crying till her eyes were all swollen up, and he gathered from Peggy's scoldings (which she did not spare him) that Susan had eaten nothing since he went away. But she was as inflexible as ever.

"Not just yet. Only not just yet. And don't say again that I do not love you," said she, suddenly hiding herself in his arms.

And so matters went on through August. The crop of oats was gathered in; the wheat-field was not ready as yet, when one fine day Michael drove up in a borrowed shandry, and offered to take Willie a ride. His manner, when Susan asked him where he was going to, was rather confused; but the answer was straight and clear enough.

He had business in Ambleside. He would never lose sight of the lad, and have him back safe and sound before dark. So Susan let him go.

Before night they were at home again: Willie in high delight at a little rattling paper windmill that Michael had bought for him in the street, and striving to imitate this new sound with perpetual buzzings. Michael, too, looked pleased. Susan knew the look, although afterwards she remembered that he had tried to veil it from her, and had assumed a grave appearance of sorrow whenever he caught her eye. He put up his horse; for, although he had three miles further to go, the moon was up—the bonny harvest-moon—and he did not care how late he had to drive on such a road by such a light. After the supper which Susan had prepared for the travellers was over, Peggy went up-stairs to see Willie safe in bed; for he had to have the same care taken of him that a little child of four years old requires.

Michael drew near to Susan.

"Susan," said he, "I took Will to see Dr. Preston, at Kendal. He's the first doctor in the county. I thought it were better for us—for you—to know at once what chance there were for him."

"Well!" said Susan, looking eagerly up. She saw the same strange glance of satisfaction, the same instant change to apparent regret and pain. "What did he say?" said she. "Speak! can't you?"

"He said he would never get better of his weakness."

"Never!"

"No; never. It's a long word, and hard to bear. And there's worse to come, dearest. The doctor thinks he will get badder from year to year. And he said, if he was us—you—he would send him off in time to Lancaster Asylum. They've ways there both of keeping such people in order and making them happy. I only tell you what he said," continued he, seeing the gathering storm in her face.

"There was no harm in his saying it," she replied, with great self-constraint, forcing herself to speak coldly instead of angrily. "Folk is welcome to their opinions."

They sat silent for a minute or two, her breast heaving with suppressed feeling.

"He's counted a very clever man," said Michael at length.

"He may be. He's none of my clever men, nor am I going to be guided by him, whatever he may think. And I don't thank them that went and took my poor lad to have such harsh notions formed about him. If I'd been there, I could have called out the sense that is in him."

"Well! I'll not say more to-night, Susan. You're not taking it rightly, and I'd best be gone, and leave you to think it over. I'll not deny they are hard words to hear, but there's sense in them, as I take it; and I reckon you'll have to come to 'em. Anyhow, it's a bad way of thanking me for my pains, and I don't take it well in you, Susan," said he, getting up, as if offended.

"Michael, I'm beside myself with sorrow. Don't blame me if I speak sharp. He and me is the only ones, you see. And mother did so charge me to have a care of him! And this is what he's come to, poor lile chap!" She began to cry, and Michael to comfort her with caresses.

"Don't," said she. "It's no use trying to make me forget poor Willie is a natural. I could hate myself for being happy with you, even for just a little minute. Go away, and leave me to face it out."

"And you'll think it over, Susan, and remember what the doctor says?"

"I can't forget," said she. She meant she could not forget what the doctor had said about the hopelessness of her brother's case; Michael had referred to the plan of sending Willie to an asylum, or madhouse, as they were called in that day and place. The idea had been gathering force in Michael's mind for some time; he had talked it over with his father, and secretly rejoiced over the possession of the farm and land which would then be his in fact, if not in law, by right of his wife. He had always considered the good penny her father could give her in his catalogue of Susan's charms and attractions. But of late he had grown to esteem her as the heiress of Yew Nook. He, too, should have land like his brother—land to possess, to cultivate, to make profit from, to bequeath. For some time he had wondered that Susan had been so much absorbed in Willie's present, that she had never seemed to look forward to his future, state. Michael had long felt the boy to be a trouble; but of late he had absolutely loathed him. His gibbering, his uncouth gestures, his loose, shambling gait, all irritated Michael inexpressibly. He did not come near the Yew Nook for a couple of days. He thought that he would leave her time to become anxious to see him and reconciled to his plan. They were strange lonely days to Susan. They were the first she had spent face to face with the sorrows that had turned her from a girl into a woman; for hitherto Michael had never let twenty-four hours pass by without coming to see her since she had had the fever. Now that he was absent, it seemed as though some cause of irritation was removed from Will, who was much more gentle and tractable than he had been for many weeks. Susan thought that she observed him making efforts at her bidding, and there was something piteous in the way in which he crept up to her, and looked wistfully in her face, as if asking her to restore him the faculties that he felt to be wanting.

"I never will let thee go, lad. Never! There's no knowing where they would take thee to, or what they would do with thee. As it says in the Bible, 'Nought but death shall part thee and me!'"

The country-side was full, in those days, of stories of the brutal treatment offered to the insane; stories that were, in fact, but too well founded, and the truth of one of which only would have been a sufficient reason for the strong prejudice existing against all such places. Each succeeding hour that Susan passed, alone, or with the poor affectionate lad for her sole companion, served to deepen her solemn resolution never to part with him. So, when Michael came, he was annoyed and surprised by the calm way in which she spoke, as if following Dr. Preston's advice was utterly and entirely out of the question. He had expected nothing less than a consent, reluctant it might be, but still a consent; and he was extremely irritated. He could have repressed his anger, but he chose rather to give way to it; thinking that he could thus best work upon Susan's affection, so as to gain his point. But, somehow, he over-reached himself; and now he was astonished in his turn at the passion of indignation that she burst into.

"Thou wilt not bide in the same house with him, say'st thou? There's no need for thy biding, as far as I can tell. There's solemn reason why I should bide with my own flesh and blood and keep to the word I pledged my mother on her death-bed; but, as for thee, there's no tie that I know on to keep thee fro' going to America or Botany Bay this very night, if that were thy inclination. I will have no more of your threats to make me send my bairn away. If thou marry me, thou'lt help me to take charge of Willie. If thou doesn't choose to marry me on those terms—why, I can snap my fingers at thee, never fear. I'm not so far gone in love as that. But I will not have thee, if thou say'st in such a hectoring way that Willie must go out of the house—and the house his own too—before thou'lt set foot in it. Willie bides here, and I bide with him."

"Thou hast may-be spoken a word too much," said Michael, pale with rage. "If I am free, as thou say'st, to go to Canada, or Botany Bay, I reckon I'm free to live where I like, and that will not be with a natural who may turn into a madman some day, for aught I know. Choose between him and me, Susy, for I swear to thee, thou shan't have both."

"I have chosen," said Susan, now perfectly composed and still. "Whatever comes of it, I bide with Willie."

"Very well," replied Michael, trying to assume an equal composure of manner. "Then I'll wish you a very good night." He went out of the house door, half-expecting to be called back again; but, instead, he heard a hasty step inside, and a bolt drawn.

"Whew!" said he to himself, "I think I must leave my lady alone for a week or two, and give her time to come to her senses. She'll not find it so easy as she thinks to let me go."

So he went past the kitchen-window in nonchalant style, and was not seen again at Yew Nook for some weeks. How did he pass the time? For the first day or two, he was unusually cross with all things and people that came athwart him. Then wheat-harvest began, and he was busy, and exultant about his heavy crop. Then a man came from a distance to bid for the lease of his farm, which, by his father's advice, had been offered for sale, as he himself was so soon likely to remove to the Yew Nook. He had so little idea that Susan really would remain firm to her determination, that he at once began to haggle with the man who came after his farm, showed him the crop just got in, and managed skilfully enough to make a good bargain for himself. Of course, the bargain had to be sealed at the public-house; and the companions he met with there soon became friends enough to tempt him into Langdale, where again he met with Eleanor Hebthwaite.

How did Susan pass the time? For the first day or so, she was too angry and offended to cry. She went about her household duties in a quick, sharp, jerking, yet absent way; shrinking one moment from Will, overwhelming him with remorseful caresses the next. The third day of Michael's absence, she had the relief of a good fit of crying; and after that, she grew softer and more tender; she felt how harshly she had spoken to him, and remembered how angry she had been. She made excuses for him. "It was no wonder," she said to herself, "that he had been vexed with her; and no wonder he would not give in, when she had never tried to speak gently or to reason with him. She was to blame, and she would tell him so, and tell him once again all that her mother had bade her to be to Willie, and all the horrible stories she had heard about madhouses, and he would be on her side at once."

And so she watched for his coming, intending to apologise as soon as ever she saw him. She hurried over her household work, in order to sit quietly at her sewing, and hear the first distant sound of his well-known step or whistle. But even the sound of her flying needle seemed too loud—perhaps she was losing an exquisite instant of anticipation; so she stopped sewing, and looked longingly out through the geranium leaves, in order that her eye might catch the first stir of the branches in the wood-path by which he generally came. Now and then a bird might spring out of the covert; otherwise the leaves were heavily still in the sultry weather of early autumn. Then she would take up her sewing, and, with a spasm of resolution, she would determine that a certain task should be fulfilled before she would again allow herself the poignant luxury of expectation. Sick at heart was she when the evening closed in, and the chances of that day diminished. Yet she stayed up longer than usual, thinking that if he were coming—if he were only passing along the distant road—the sight of a light in the window might encourage him to make his appearance even at that late hour, while seeing the house all darkened and shut up might quench any such intention.

Very sick and weary at heart, she went to bed; too desolate and despairing to cry, or make any moan. But in the morning hope came afresh. Another day—another chance! And so it went on for weeks. Peggy understood her young mistress's sorrow full well, and respected it by her silence on the subject. Willie seemed happier now that the irritation of Michael's presence was removed; for the poor idiot had a sort of antipathy to Michael, which was a kind of heart's echo to the repugnance in which the latter held him. Altogether, just at this time, Willie was the happiest of the three.

As Susan went into Coniston, to sell her butter, one Saturday, some inconsiderate person told her that she had seen Michael Hurst the night before. I said inconsiderate, but I might rather have said unobservant; for any one who had spent half-an-hour in Susan Dixon's company might have seen that she disliked having any reference made to the subjects nearest her heart, were they joyous or grievous. Now she went a little paler than usual (and she had never recovered her colour since she had had the fever), and tried to keep silence. But an irrepressible pang forced out the question—

"Where?"

"At Thomas Applethwaite's, in Langdale. They had a kind of harvest-home, and he were there among the young folk, and very thick wi' Nelly Hebthwaite, old Thomas's niece. Thou'lt have to look after him a bit, Susan!"

She neither smiled nor sighed. The neighbour who had been speaking to her was struck with the gray stillness of her face. Susan herself felt how well her self-command was obeyed by every little muscle, and said to herself in her Spartan manner, "I can bear it without either wincing or blenching." She went home early, at a tearing, passionate pace, trampling and breaking through all obstacles of briar or bush. Willie was moping in her absence—hanging listlessly on the farm-yard gate to watch for her. When he saw her, he set up one of his strange, inarticulate cries, of which she was now learning the meaning, and came towards her with his loose, galloping run, head and limbs all shaking and wagging with pleasant excitement. Suddenly she turned from him, and burst into tears. She sat down on a stone by the wayside, not a hundred yards from home, and buried her face in her hands, and gave way to a passion of pent-up sorrow; so terrible and full of agony were her low cries, that the idiot stood by her, aghast and silent. All his joy gone for the time, but not, like her joy, turned into ashes. Some thought struck him. Yes! the sight of her woe made him think, great as the exertion was. He ran, and stumbled, and shambled home, buzzing with his lips all the time. She never missed him. He came back in a trice, bringing with him his cherished paper windmill, bought on that fatal day when Michael had taken him into Kendal to have his doom of perpetual idiocy pronounced. He thrust it into Susan's face, her hands, her lap, regardless of the injury his frail plaything thereby received. He leapt before her to think how he had cured all heart-sorrow, buzzing louder than ever. Susan looked up at him, and that glance of her sad eyes sobered him. He began to whimper, he knew not why: and she now, comforter in her turn, tried to soothe him by twirling his windmill. But it was broken; it made no noise; it would not go round. This seemed to afflict Susan more than him. She tried to make it right, although she saw the task was hopeless; and while she did so, the tears rained down unheeded from her bent head on the paper toy.

"It won't do," said she, at last. "It will never do again." And, somehow, she took the accident and her words as omens of the love that was broken, and that she feared could never be pieced together more. She rose up and took Willie's hand, and the two went slowly into the house.

To her surprise, Michael Hurst sat in the house-place. House-place is a sort of better kitchen, where no cookery is done, but which is reserved for state occasions. Michael had gone in there because he was accompanied by his only sister, a woman older than himself, who was well married beyond Keswick, and who now came for the first time to make acquaintance with Susan. Michael had primed his sister with his wishes regarding Will, and the position in which he stood with Susan; and arriving at Yew Nook in the absence of the latter, he had not scrupled to conduct his sister into the guest-room, as he held Mrs. Gale's worldly position in respect and admiration, and therefore wished her to be favourably impressed with all the signs of property which he was beginning to consider as Susan's greatest charms. He had secretly said to himself, that if Eleanor Hebthwaite and Susan Dixon were equal in point of riches, he would sooner have Eleanor by far. He had begun to consider Susan as a termagant; and when he thought of his intercourse with her, recollections of her somewhat warm and hasty temper came far more readily to his mind than any remembrance of her generous, loving nature.

And now she stood face to face with him; her eyes tear-swollen, her garments dusty, and here and there torn in consequence of her rapid progress through the bushy by-paths. She did not make a favourable impression on the well-clad Mrs. Gale, dressed in her best silk gown, and therefore unusually susceptible to the appearance of another. Nor were Susan's manners gracious or cordial. How could they be, when she remembered what had passed between Michael and herself the last time they met? For her penitence had faded away under the daily disappointment of these last weary weeks.

But she was hospitable in substance. She bade Peggy hurry on the kettle, and busied herself among the tea-cups, thankful that the presence of Mrs. Gale, as a stranger, would prevent the immediate recurrence to the one subject which she felt must be present in Michael's mind as well as in her own. But Mrs. Gale was withheld by no such feelings of delicacy. She had come ready-primed with the case, and had undertaken to bring the girl to reason. There was no time to be lost. It had been prearranged between the brother and sister that he was to stroll out into the farm-yard before his sister introduced the subject; but she was so confident in the success of her arguments, that she must needs have the triumph of a victory as soon as possible; and, accordingly, she brought a hail-storm of good reasons to bear upon Susan. Susan did not reply for a long time; she was so indignant at this intermeddling of a stranger in the deep family sorrow and shame. Mrs. Gale thought she was gaining the day, and urged her arguments more pitilessly. Even Michael winced for Susan, and wondered at her silence. He shrank out of sight, and into the shadow, hoping that his sister might prevail, but annoyed at the hard way in which she kept putting the case.

Suddenly Susan turned round from the occupation she had pretended to be engaged in, and said to him in a low voice, which yet not only vibrated itself, but made its hearers thrill through all their obtuseness:

"Michael Hurst! does your sister speak truth, think you?"

Both women looked at him for his answer; Mrs. Gale without anxiety, for had she not said the very words they had spoken together before? had she not used the very arguments that he himself had suggested? Susan, on the contrary, looked to his answer as settling her doom for life; and in the gloom of her eyes you might have read more despair than hope.

He shuffled his position. He shuffled in his words.

"What is it you ask? My sister has said many things."

"I ask you," said Susan, trying to give a crystal clearness both to her expressions and her pronunciation, "if, knowing as you do how Will is afflicted, you will help me to take that charge of him which I promised my mother on her death-bed that I would do; and which means, that I shall keep him always with me, and do all in my power to make his life happy. If you will do this, I will be your wife; if not, I remain unwed."

"But he may get dangerous; he can be but a trouble; his being here is a pain to you, Susan, not a pleasure."

"I ask you for either yes or no," said she, a little contempt at his evading her question mingling with her tone. He perceived it, and it nettled him.

"And I have told you. I answered your question the last time I was here. I said I would ne'er keep house with an idiot; no more I will. So now you've gotten your answer."

"I have," said Susan. And she sighed deeply.

"Come, now," said Mrs. Gale, encouraged by the sigh; "one would think you don't love Michael, Susan, to be so stubborn in yielding to what I'm sure would be best for the lad."

"Oh! she does not care for me," said Michael. "I don't believe she ever did."

"Don't I? Haven't I?" asked Susan, her eyes blazing out fire. She left the room directly, and sent Peggy in to make the tea; and catching at Will, who was lounging about in the kitchen, she went up-stairs with him and bolted herself in, straining the boy to her heart, and keeping almost breathless, lest any noise she made might cause him to break out into the howls and sounds which she could not bear that those below should hear.

A knock at the door. It was Peggy.

"He wants for to see you, to wish you good-bye."

"I cannot come. Oh, Peggy, send them away."

It was her only cry for sympathy; and the old servant understood it. She sent them away, somehow; not politely, as I have been given to understand.

"Good go with them," said Peggy, as she grimly watched their retreating figures. "We're rid of bad rubbish, anyhow." And she turned into the house, with the intention of making ready some refreshment for Susan, after her hard day at the market, and her harder evening. But in the kitchen, to which she passed through the empty house-place, making a face of contemptuous dislike at the used tea-cups and fragments of a meal yet standing there, she found Susan, with her sleeves tucked up and her working apron on, busied in preparing to make clap-bread, one of the hardest and hottest domestic tasks of a Daleswoman. She looked up, and first met, and then avoided Peggy's eye; it was too full of sympathy. Her own cheeks were flushed, and her own eyes were dry and burning.

"Where's the board, Peggy? We need clap-bread; and, I reckon, I've time to get through with it to-night." Her voice had a sharp, dry tone in it, and her motions a jerking angularity about them.

Peggy said nothing, but fetched her all that she needed. Susan beat her cakes thin with vehement force. As she stooped over them, regardless even of the task in which she seemed so much occupied, she was surprised by a touch on her mouth of something—what she did not see at first. It was a cup of tea, delicately sweetened and cooled, and held to her lips, when exactly ready, by the faithful old woman. Susan held it off a hand's breath, and looked into Peggy's eyes, while her own filled with the strange relief of tears.

"Lass!" said Peggy, solemnly, "thou hast done well. It is not long to bide, and then the end will come."

"But you are very old, Peggy," said Susan, quivering.

"It is but a day sin' I were young," replied Peggy; but she stopped the conversation by again pushing the cup with gentle force to Susan's dry and thirsty lips. When she had drunken she fell again to her labour, Peggy heating the hearth, and doing all that she knew would be required, but never speaking another word. Willie basked close to the fire, enjoying the animal luxury of warmth, for the autumn evenings were beginning to be chilly. It was one o'clock before they thought of going to bed on that memorable night.

CHAPTER IV

THE vehemence with which Susan Dixon threw herself into occupation could not last for ever. Times of languor and remembrance would come—times when she recurred with a passionate yearning to bygone days, the recollection of which was so vivid and delicious, that it seemed as though it were the reality, and the present bleak bareness the dream. She smiled anew at the magical sweetness of some touch or tone which in memory she felt and heard, and drank the delicious cup of poison, although at the very time she knew what the consequences of racking pain would be.

"This time, last year," thought she, "we went nutting together—this very day last year; just such a day as to-day. Purple and gold were the lights on the hills; the leaves were just turning brown; here and there on the sunny slopes the stubble-fields looked tawny; down in a cleft of yon purple slate-rock the beck fell like a silver glancing thread; all just as it is to-day. And he climbed the slender, swaying nut-trees, and bent the branches for me to gather; or made a passage through the hazel copses, from time to time claiming a toll. Who could have thought he loved me so little?—who?—who?"

Or, as the evening closed in, she would allow herself to imagine that she heard his coming step, just that she might recall time feeling of exquisite delight which had passed by without the due and passionate relish at the time. Then she would wonder how she could have had strength, the cruel, self-piercing strength, to say what she had done; to stab himself with that stern resolution, of which the sear would remain till her dying day. It might have been right; but, as she sickened, she wished she had not instinctively chosen the right. How luxurious a life haunted by no stern sense of duty must be! And many led this kind of life; why could not she? O, for one hour again of his sweet company! If he came now, she would agree to whatever he proposed.

It was a fever of the mind. She passed through it, and came out healthy, if weak. She was capable once more of taking pleasure in following an unseen guide through briar and brake. She returned with tenfold affection to her protecting care of Willie. She acknowledged to herself that he was to be her all-in-all in life. She made him her constant companion. For his sake, as the real owner of Yew Nook, and she as his steward and guardian, she began that course of careful saving, and that love of acquisition, which afterwards gained for her the reputation of being miserly. She still thought that he might regain a scanty portion of sense—enough to require some simple pleasures and excitement, which would cost money. And money should not be wanting. Peggy rather assisted her in the formation of her parsimonious habits than otherwise; economy was the order of the district, and a certain degree of respectable avarice the characteristic of her age. Only Willie was never stinted nor hindered of anything that the two women thought could give him pleasure, for want of money.

There was one gratification which Susan felt was needed for the restoration of her mind to its more healthy state, after she had passed through the whirling fever, when duty was as nothing, and anarchy reigned; a gratification that, somehow, was to be her last burst of unreasonableness; of which she knew and recognised pain as the sure consequence. She must see him once more,—herself unseen.

The week before the Christmas of this memorable year, she went out in the dusk of the early winter evening, wrapped close in shawl and cloak. She wore her dark shawl under her cloak, putting it over her head in lieu of a bonnet; for she knew that she might have to wait long in concealment. Then she tramped over the wet fell-path, shut in by misty rain for miles and miles, till she came to the place where he was lodging; a farm-house in Langdale, with a steep, stony lane leading up to it: this lane was entered by a gate out of the main road, and by the gate were a few bushes—thorns; but of them the leaves had fallen, and they offered no concealment: an old wreck of a yew-tree grew among them, however, and underneath that Susan cowered down, shrouding her face, of which the colour might betray her, with a corner of her shawl. Long did she wait; cold and cramped she became, too damp and stiff to change her posture readily. And after all, he might never come! But, she would wait till daylight, if need were; and she pulled out a crust, with which she had providently supplied herself. The rain had ceased,—a dull, still, brooding weather had succeeded; it was a night to hear distant sounds. She heard horses' hoofs striking and splashing in the stones, and in the pools of the road at her back. Two horses; not well-ridden, or evenly guided, as she could tell.

Michael Hurst and a companion drew near: not tipsy, but not sober. They stopped at the gate to bid each other a maudlin farewell. Michael stooped forward to catch the latch with the hook of the stick which he carried; he dropped the stick, and it fell with one end close to Susan,—indeed, with the slightest change of posture she could have opened the gate for him. He swore a great oath, and struck his horse with his closed fist, as if that animal had been to blame; then he dismounted, opened the gate, and fumbled about for his stick. When he had found it (Susan had touched the other end) his first use of it was to flog his horse well, and she had much ado to avoid its kicks and plunges. Then, still swearing, he staggered up the lane, for it was evident he was not sober enough to remount.

By daylight Susan was back and at her daily labours at Yew Nook. When the spring came, Michael Hurst was married to Eleanor Hebthwaite. Others, too, were married, and christenings made their firesides merry and glad; or they travelled, and came back after long years with many wondrous tales. More rarely, perhaps, a Dalesman changed his dwelling. But to all households more change came than to Yew Nook. There the seasons came round with monotonous sameness; or, if they brought mutation, it was of a slow, and decaying, and depressing kind. Old Peggy died. Her silent sympathy, concealed under much roughness, was a loss to Susan Dixon. Susan was not yet thirty when this happened, but she looked a middle-aged, not to say an elderly woman. People affirmed that she had never recovered her complexion since that fever, a dozen years ago, which killed her father, and left Will Dixon an idiot. But besides her gray sallowness, the lines in her face were strong, and deep, and hard. The movements of her eyeballs were slow and heavy; the wrinkles at the corners of her mouth and eyes were planted firm and sure; not an ounce of unnecessary flesh was there on her bones—every muscle started strong and ready for use. She needed all this bodily strength, to a degree that no human creature, now Peggy was dead, knew of: for Willie had grown up large and strong in body, and, in general, docile enough in mind; but, every now and then, he became first moody, and then violent. These paroxysms lasted but a day or two; and it was Susan's anxious care to keep their very existence hidden and unknown. It is true, that occasional passers-by on that lonely road heard sounds at night of knocking about of furniture, blows, and cries, as of some tearing demon within the solitary farm-house; but these fits of violence usually occurred in the night; and whatever had been their consequence, Susan had tidied and redded up all signs of aught unusual before the morning. For, above all, she dreaded lest some one might find out in what danger and peril she occasionally was, and might assume a right to take away her brother from her care. The one idea of taking charge of him had deepened and deepened with years. It was graven into her mind as the object for which she lived. The sacrifice she had made for this object only made it more precious to her. Besides, she separated the idea of the docile, affectionate, loutish, indolent Will, and kept it distinct from the terror which the demon that occasionally possessed him inspired her with. The one was her flesh and her blood—the child of her dead mother; the other was some fiend who came to torture and convulse the creature she so loved. She believed that she fought her brother's battle in holding down those tearing hands, in binding whenever she could those uplifted restless arms prompt and prone to do mischief. All the time she subdued him with her cunning or her strength, she spoke to him in pitying murmurs, or abused the third person, the fiendish enemy, in no unmeasured tones. Towards morning the paroxysm was exhausted, and he would fall asleep, perhaps only to waken with evil and renewed vigour. But when he was laid down, she would sally out to taste the fresh air, and to work off her wild sorrow in cries and mutterings to herself. The early labourers saw her gestures at a distance, and thought her as crazed as the idiot-brother who made the neighbourhood a haunted place. But did any chance person call at Yew Nook later on in the day, he would find Susan Dixon cold, calm, collected; her manner curt, her wits keen.

Once this fit of violence lasted longer than usual. Susan's strength both of mind and body was nearly worn out; she wrestled in prayer that somehow it might end before she, too, was driven mad; or, worse, might be obliged to give up life's aim, and consign Willie to a madhouse. From that moment of prayer (as she afterwards superstitiously thought) Willie calmed—and then he drooped—and then he sank—and, last of all, he died in reality from physical exhaustion.

But he was so gentle and tender as he lay on his dying bed; such strange, child-like gleams of returning intelligence came over his face, long after the power to make his dull, inarticulate sounds had departed, that Susan was attracted to him by a stronger tie than she had ever felt before. It was something to have even an idiot loving her with dumb, wistful, animal affection; something to have any creature looking at her with such beseeching eyes, imploring protection from the insidious enemy stealing on. And yet she knew that to him death was no enemy, but a true friend, restoring light and health to his poor clouded mind. It was to her that death was an enemy; to her, the survivor, when Willie died; there was no one to love her.

Worse doom still, there was no one left on earth for her to love.

You now know why no wandering tourist could persuade her to receive him as a lodger; why no tired traveller could melt her heart to afford him rest and refreshment; why long habits of seclusion had given her a moroseness of manner, and how care for the interests of another had rendered her keen and miserly.

But there was a third act in the drama of her life.

CHAPTER V

IN spite of Peggy's prophecy that Susan's life should not seem long, it did seem wearisome and endless, as the years slowly uncoiled their monotonous circles. To be sure, she might have made change for herself, but she did not care to do it. It was, indeed, more than "not caring," which merely implies a certain degree of vis inertiæ to be subdued before an object can be attained, and that the object itself does not seem to be of sufficient importance to call out the requisite energy. On the contrary, Susan exerted herself to avoid change and variety. She had a morbid dread of new faces, which originated in her desire to keep poor dead Willie's state a profound secret. She had a contempt for new customs; and, indeed, her old ways prospered so well under her active hand and vigilant eye, that it was difficult to know how they could be improved upon. She was regularly present in Coniston market with the best butter and the earliest chickens of the season. Those were the common farm produce that every farmer's wife about had to sell; but Susan, after she had disposed of the more feminine articles, turned to on the man's side. A better judge of a horse or cow there was not in all the country round. Yorkshire itself might have attempted to jockey her, and would have failed. Her corn was sound and clean; her potatoes well preserved to the latest spring. People began to talk of the hoards of money Susan Dixon must have laid up somewhere; and one young ne'er-do-weel of a farmer's son undertook to make love to the woman of forty, who looked fifty-five, if a day. He made up to her by opening a gate on the road-path home, as she was riding on a bare-backed horse, her purchase not an hour ago. She was off before him, refusing his civility; but the remounting was not so easy, and rather than fail she did not choose to attempt it. She walked, and he walked alongside, improving his opportunity, which, as he vainly thought, had been consciously granted to him. As they drew near Yew Nook, he ventured on some expression of a wish to keep company with her. His words were vague and clumsily arranged. Susan turned round and coolly asked him to explain himself, he took courage, as he thought of her reputed wealth, and expressed his wishes this second time pretty plainly. To his surprise, the reply she made was in a series of smart strokes across his shoulders, administered through the medium of a supple hazel-switch.

"Take that!" said she, almost breathless, "to teach thee how thou darest make a fool of an honest woman old enough to be thy mother. If thou com'st a step nearer the house, there's a good horse-pool, and there's two stout fellows who'll like no better fun than ducking thee. Be off wi' thee!"

And she strode into her own premises, never looking round to see whether he obeyed her injunction or not.

Sometimes three or four years would pass over without her hearing Michael Hurst's name mentioned. She used to wonder at such times whether he were dead or alive. She would sit for hours by the dying embers of her fire on a winter's evening, trying to recall the scenes of her youth; trying to bring up living pictures of the faces she had then known—Michael's most especially. She thought it was possible, so long had been the lapse of years, that she might now pass by him in the street unknowing and unknown. His outward form she might not recognize, but himself she should feel in the thrill of her whole being. He could not pass her unawares.

What little she did hear about him, all testified a downward tendency. He drank—not at stated times when there was no other work to be done, but continually, whether it was seed-time or harvest. His children were all ill at the same time; then one died, while the others recovered, but were poor sickly things. No one dared to give Susan any direct intelligence of her former lover; many avoided all mention of his name in her presence; but a few spoke out either in indifference to, or ignorance of, those bygone days. Susan heard every word, every whisper, every sound that related to him. But her eye never changed, nor did a muscle of her face move.

Late one November night she sat over her fire; not a human being besides herself in the house; none but she had ever slept there since Willie's death. The farm-labourers had foddered the cattle and gone home hours before. There were crickets chirping all round the warm hearth-stones; there was the clock ticking with the peculiar beat Susan had known from her childhood, and which then and ever since she had oddly associated within the idea of a mother and child talking together, one loud tick, and quick—a feeble, sharp one following.

The day had been keen, and piercingly cold. The whole lift of heaven seemed a dome of iron. Black and frost-bound was the earth under the cruel east wind. Now the wind had dropped, and as the darkness had gathered in, the weather-wise old labourers prophesied snow. The sounds in the air arose again, as Susan sat still and silent. They were of a different character to what they had been during the prevalence of the east wind. Then they had been shrill and piping; now they were like low distant growling; not unmusical, but strangely threatening. Susan went to the window, and drew aside the little curtain. The whole world was white—the air was blinded with the swift and heavy fall of snow. At present it came down straight, but Susan knew those distant sounds in the hollows and gulleys of the hills portended a driving wind and a more cruel storm. She thought of her sheep; were they all folded? the new-born calf, was it bedded well? Before the drifts were formed too deep for her to pass in and out—and by the morning she judged that they would be six or seven feet deep—she would go out and see after the comfort of her beasts. She took a lantern, and tied a shawl over her head, and went out into the open air. She had tenderly provided for all her animals, and was returning, when, borne on the blast as if some spirit-cry—for it seemed to come rather down from the skies than from any creature standing on earth's level—she heard a voice of agony; she could not distinguish words; it seemed rather as if some bird of prey was being caught in the whirl of the icy wind, and torn and tortured by its violence. Again up high above! Susan put down her lantern, and shouted loud in return; it was an instinct, for if the creature were not human, which she had doubted but a moment before, what good could her responding cry do? And her cry was seized on by the tyrannous wind, and borne farther away in the opposite direction to that from which the call of agony had proceeded. Again she listened; no sound: then again it rang through space; and this time she was sure it was human. She turned into the house, and heaped turf and wood on the fire, which, careless of her own sensations, she had allowed to fade and almost die out. She put a new candle in her lantern; she changed her shawl for a maud, and leaving the door on latch, she sallied out. Just at the moment when her ear first encountered the weird noises of the storm, on issuing forth into the open air, she thought she heard the words, "O God! O help!" They were a guide to her, if words they were, for they came straight from a rock not a quarter of a mile from Yew Nook, but only to be reached, on account of its precipitous character, by a round-about path. Thither she steered, defying wind and snow; guided by here a thorn-tree, there an old, doddered oak, which had not quite lest their identity under the whelming mask of snow. Now and then she stopped to listen; but never a word or sound heard she, till right from where the copse-wood grew thick and tangled at the base of the rock, round which she was winding, she heard a moan. Into the brake— all snow in appearance—almost a plain of snow looked on from the little eminence where she stood— she plunged, breaking down the bush, stumbling, bruising herself, fighting her way; her lantern held between her teeth, and she herself using head as well as hands to butt away a passage, at whatever cost of bodily injury. As she climbed or staggered, owing to the unevenness of the snow-covered ground, where the briars and weeds of years were tangled and matted together, her foot felt something strangely soft and yielding. She lowered her lantern; there lay a man, prone on his face, nearly covered by the fast-falling flakes; he must have fallen from the rock above, as, not knowing of the circuitous path, he had tried to descend its steep, slippery face. Who could tell? it was no time for thinking. Susan lifted him up with her wiry strength; he gave no help—no sign of life; but for all that he might be alive: he was still warm; she tied her maud round him; she fastened the lantern to her apron-string; she held him tight: half-carrying, half-dragging—what did a few bruises signify to him, compared to dear life, to precious life! She got him through the brake, and down the path. There, for an instant, she stopped to take breath; but, as if stung by the Furies, she pushed on again with almost superhuman strength. Clasping him round the waist, and leaning his dead weight against the lintel of the door, she tried to undo the latch; but now, just at this moment, a trembling faintness came over her, and a fearful dread took possession of her—that here, on the very threshold of her home, she might be found dead, and buried under the snow, when the farm-servants came in the morning. This terror stirred her up to one more effort. Then she and her companion were in the warmth of the quiet haven of that kitchen; she laid him on the settle, and sank on the floor by his side. How long she remained in this swoon she could not tell; not very long she judged by the fire, which was still red and sullenly glowing when she came to herself. She lighted the candle, and bent over her late burden to ascertain if indeed he were dead. She stood long gazing. The man lay dead. There could be no doubt about it. His filmy eyes glared at her, unshut. But Susan was not one to be affrighted by the stony aspect of death. It was not that; it was the bitter, woeful recognition of Michael Hurst!

She was convinced he was dead; but after a while she refused to believe in her conviction. She stripped off his wet outer-garments with trembling, hurried hands. She brought a blanket down from her own bed; she made up the fire. She swathed him in fresh, warm wrappings, and laid him on the flags before the fire, sitting herself at his head, and holding it in her lap, while she tenderly wiped his loose, wet hair, curly still, although its colour had changed from nut-brown to iron-gray since she had seen it last. From time to time she bent over the face afresh, sick, and fain to believe that the flicker of the fire-light was some slight convulsive motion. But the dim, staring eyes struck chill to her heart. At last she ceased her delicate, busy cares: but she still held the head softly, as if caressing it. She thought over all the possibilities and chances in the mingled yarn of their lives that might, by so slight a turn, have ended far otherwise. If her mother's cold had been early tended, so that the responsibility as to her brother's weal or woe had not fallen upon her; if the fever had not taken such rough, cruel hold on Will; nay, if Mrs. Gale, that hard, worldly sister, had not accompanied him on his last visit to Yew Nook—his very last before this fatal, stormy might; if she had heard his cry,—cry uttered by these pale, dead lips with such wild, despairing agony, not yet three hours ago!—O! if she had but heard it sooner, he might have been saved before that blind, false step had precipitated him down the rock! In going over this weary chain of unrealized possibilities, Susan learnt the force of Peggy's words. Life was short, looking back upon it. It seemed but yesterday since all the love of her being had been poured out, and run to waste. The intervening years—the long monotonous years that had turned her into an old woman before her time—were but a dream.

The labourers coming in the dawn of the winter's day were surprised to see the fire-light through the low kitchen-window. They knocked, and hearing a moaning answer, they entered, fearing that something had befallen their mistress. For all explanation they got these words

"It is Michael Hurst. He was belated, and fell down the Raven's Crag. Where does Eleanor, his wife, live?"

How Michael Hurst got to Yew Nook no one but Susan ever knew. They thought he had dragged himself there, with some sore internal bruise sapping away his minuted life. They could not have believed the superhuman exertion which had first sought him out, and then dragged him hither. Only Susan knew of that.

She gave him into the charge of her servants, and went out and saddled her horse. Where the wind had drifted the snow on one side, and the road was clear and bare, she rode, and rode fast; where the soft, deceitful heaps were massed up, she dismounted and led her steed, plunging in deep, with fierce energy, the pain at her heart urging her onwards with a sharp, digging spur.

The gray, solemn, winter's noon was more night-like than the depth of summer's night; dim-purple brooded the low skies over the white earth, as Susan rode up to what had been Michael Hurst's abode while living. It was a small farm-house carelessly kept outside, slatternly tended within. The pretty Nelly Hebthwaite was pretty still; her delicate face had never suffered from any long-enduring feeling. If anything, its expression was that of plaintive sorrow; but the soft, light hair had scarcely a tinge of gray; the wood-rose tint of complexion yet remained, if not so brilliant as in youth; the straight nose, the small mouth were untouched by time. Susan felt the contrast even at that moment. She knew that her own skin was weather-beaten, furrowed, brown,—that her teeth were gone, and her hair gray and ragged. And yet she was not two years older than Nelly,—she had not been, in youth, when she took account of these things. Nelly stood wondering at the strange-enough horse-woman, who stopped and panted at the door, holding her horse's bridle, and refusing to enter.

"Where is Michael Hurst?" asked Susan, at last.

"Well, I can't rightly say. He should have been at home last night, but he was off, seeing after a public-house to be let at Ulverstone, for our farm does not answer, and we were thinking—"

"He did not come home last night?" said Susan, cutting short the story, and half-affirming, half-questioning, by way of letting in a ray of the awful light before she let it full in, in its consuming wrath.

"No! he'll be stopping somewhere out Ulverstone ways. I'm sure we've need of him at home, for I've no one but lile Tommy to help me tend the beasts. Things have not gone well with us, and we don't keep a servant now. But you're trembling all over, ma'am. You'd better come in, and take something warm, while your horse rests. That's the stable-door, to your left."

Susan took her horse there; loosened his girths, and rubbed him down with a wisp of straw. Then she hooked about her for hay; but the place was bare of feed, and smelt damp and unused. She went to the house, thankful for the respite, and got some clap-bread, which she mashed up in a pailful of lukewarm water. Every moment was a respite, and yet every moment made her dread the more the task that lay before her. It would be longer than she thought at first. She took the saddle off, and hung about her horse, which seemed, somehow, more like a friend than anything else in the world. She laid her cheek against its neck, and rested there, before returning to the house for the last time.

Eleanor had brought down one of her own gowns, which hung on a chair against the fire, and had made her unknown visitor a cup of hot tea. Susan could hardly bear all these little attentions: they choked her, and yet she was so wet, so weak with fatigue and excitement, that she could neither resist by voice or by action. Two children stood awkwardly about, puzzled at the scene, and even Eleanor began to wish for some explanation of who her strange visitor was.

"You've, maybe, heard him speaking of me? I'm called Susan Dixon."

Nelly coloured, and avoided meeting Susan's eye.

"I've heard other folk speak of you. He never named your name."

This respect of silence came like balm to Susan: balm not felt or heeded at the time it was applied, but very grateful in its effects for all that.

"He is at my house," continued Susan, determined not to stop or quaver in the operation—the pain which must be inflicted.

"At your house? Yew Nook?" questioned Eleanor, surprised. "How came he there?"—half jealously. "Did he take shelter from the coming storm? Tell me,—there is something—tell me, woman!"

"He took no shelter. Would to God he had!"

"O! would to God! would to God!" shrieked out Eleanor, learning all from the woful import of those dreary eyes. Her cries thrilled through the house; the children's piping wailings and passionate cries on "Daddy! Daddy!" pierced into Susan's very marrow. But she remained as still and tearless as the great round face upon the clock.

At last, in a lull of crying, she said,—not exactly questioning, but as if partly to herself—

"You loved him, then?"

"Loved him! he was my husband! He was the father of three bonny bairns that lie dead in Grasmere churchyard. I wish you'd go, Susan Dixon, and let me weep without your watching me! I wish you'd never come near the place."

"Alas! alas! it would not have brought him to life. I would have laid down my own to save his. My life has been so very sad! No one would have cared if I had died. Alas! alas!"

The tone in which she said this was so utterly mournful and despairing that it awed Nelly into quiet for a time. But by-and-by she said, "I would not turn a dog out to do it harm; but the night is clear, and Tommy shall guide you to the Red Cow. But, oh, I want to be alone! If you'll come back to-morrow, I'll be better, and I'll hear all, and thank you for every kindness you have shown him,—and I do believe you've showed him kindness,—though I don't know why."

Susan moved heavily and strangely.

She said something—her words came thick and unintelligible. She had had a paralytic stroke since she had last spoken. She could not go, even if she would. Nor did Eleanor, when she became aware of the state of the case, wish her to leave. She had her laid on her own bed, and weeping silently all the while for her lost husband, she nursed Susan like a sister. She did not know what her guest's worldly position might be; and she might never be repaid. But she sold many a little trifle to purchase such small comforts as Susan needed. Susan, lying still and motionless, learnt much. It was not a severe stroke; it might be the forerunner of others yet to come, but at some distance of time. But for the present she recovered, and regained much of her former health. On her sick-bed she matured her plans. When she returned to Yew Nook, she took Michael Hurst's widow and children with her to live there, and fill up the haunted hearth with living forms that should banish the ghosts.

And so it fell out that the latter days of Susan Dixon's life were better than the former.

THE DOOM OF THE GRIFFITHS

CHAPTER I

I HAVE always been much interested by the traditions which are scattered up and down North Wales relating to Owen Glendower (Owain Glendwr is the national spelling of the name), and I fully enter into the feeling which makes the Welsh peasant still look upon him as the hero of his country. There was great joy among many of the inhabitants of the principality, when the subject of the Welsh prize poem at Oxford, some fifteen or sixteen years ago, was announced to be "Owain Glendwr." It was the most proudly national subject that had been given for years.

Perhaps, some may not be aware that this redoubted chieftain is, even in the present days of enlightenment, as famous among his illiterate countrymen for his magical powers as for his patriotism. He says himself—or Shakespeare says it for him, which is much the same thing—

'At my nativity
The front of heaven was full of fiery shapes
Of burning cressets . . .   . . .
I can call spirits from the vasty deep.'

And few among the lower orders in the principality would think of asking Hotspur's irreverent question in reply.

Among other traditions preserved relative to this part of the Welsh hero's character, is the old family prophecy which gives title to this tale. When Sir David Gam, "as black a traitor as if he had been born in Builth," sought to murder Owen at Machynlleth, there was one with him whose name Glendwr little dreamed of having associated with his enemies. Rhys ap Gryfydd, his "old familiar friend," his relation, his more than brother, had consented unto his blood. Sir David Gam might be forgiven, but one whom he had loved, and who had betrayed him, could never be forgiven. Glendwr was too deeply read in the human heart to kill him. No, he let him live on, the loathing and scorn of his compatriots, and the victim of bitter remorse. The mark of Cain was upon him.

But before he went forth—while he yet stood a prisoner, cowering beneath his conscience before Owain Glendwr—that chieftain passed a doom upon him and his race:

"I doom thee to live, because I know thou wilt pray for death. Thou shalt live on beyond the natural term of the life of man, the scorn of all good men. The very children shall point to thee with hissing tongue, and say, 'There goes one who would have shed a brother's blood!' For I loved thee more than a brother, oh Rhys ap Gryfydd! Thou shalt live on to see all of thy house, except the weakling in arms, perish by the sword. Thy race shall be accursed. Each generation shall see their lands melt away like snow; yea their wealth shall vanish, though they may labour night and day to heap up gold. And when nine generations have passed from the face of the earth, thy blood shall no longer flow in the veins of any human being. In those days the last male of thy race shall avenge me. The son shall slay the father."

Such was the traditionary account of Owain Glendwr's speech to his once-trusted friend. And it was declared that the doom had been fulfilled in all things; that live in as miserly a manner as they would, the Griffiths never were wealthy and prosperous—indeed that their worldly stock diminished without any visible cause.

But the lapse of many years had almost deadened the wonder-inspiring power of the whole curse. It was only brought forth from the hoards of Memory when some untoward event happened to the Griffiths family; and in the eighth generation the faith in the prophecy was nearly destroyed, by the marriage of the Griffiths of that day, to a Miss Owen, who, unexpectedly, by the death of a brother, became an heiress—to no considerable amount, to be sure, but enough to make the prophecy appear reversed. The heiress and her husband removed from his small patrimonial estate in Merionethshire, to her heritage in Caernarvonshire, and for a time the prophecy lay dormant.

If you go from Tremadoc to Criccaeth, you pass by the parochial church of Ynysynhanarn, situated in a boggy valley running from the mountains, which shoulder up to the Rivals, down to Cardigan Bay. This tract of land has every appearance of having been redeemed at no distant period of time from the sea, and has all the desolate rankness often attendant upon such marshes. But the valley beyond, similar in character, had yet more of gloom at the time of which I write. In the higher part there were large plantations of firs, set too closely to attain any size, and remaining stunted in height and scrubby in appearance. Indeed, many of the smaller and more weakly had died, and the bark had fallen down on the brown soil neglected and unnoticed. These trees had a ghastly appearance, with their white trunks, seen by the dim light which struggled through the thick boughs above. Nearer to the sea, the valley assumed a more open, though hardly a more cheerful character; it looked dark and overhung by sea-fog through the greater part of the year, and even a farm-house, which usually imparts something of cheerfulness to a landscape, failed to do so here. This valley formed the greater part of the estate to which Owen Griffiths became entitled by right of his wife. In the higher part of the valley was situated the family mansion, or rather dwelling-house, for "mansion" is too grand a word to apply to the clumsy, but substantially-built Bodowen. It was square and heavy-looking, with just that much pretension to ornament necessary to distinguish it from the mere farm-house.

In this dwelling Mrs. Owen Griffiths bore her husband two sons—Llewellyn, the future Squire, and Robert, who was early destined for the Church. The only difference in their situation, up to the time when Robert was entered at Jesus College, was, that the elder was invariably indulged by all around him, while Robert was thwarted and indulged by turns; that Llewellyn never learned anything from the poor Welsh parson, who was nominally his private tutor; while occasionally Squire Griffiths made a great point of enforcing Robert's diligence, telling him that, as he had his bread to earn, he must pay attention to his learning. There is no knowing how far the very irregular education he had received would have carried Robert through his college examinations; but, luckily for him in this respect, before such a trial of his learning came round, he heard of the death of his elder brother, after a short illness, brought on by a hard drinking-bout. Of course, Robert was summoned home, and it seemed quite as much of course, now that there was no necessity for him to "earn his bread by his learning," that he should not return to Oxford. So the half-educated, but not unintelligent, young man continued at home, during the short remainder of his parent's lifetime.

His was not an uncommon character. In general he was mild, indolent, and easily managed; but once thoroughly roused, his passions were vehement and fearful. He seemed, indeed, almost afraid of himself, and in common hardly dared to give way to justifiable anger—so much did he dread losing his self-control. Had he been judiciously educated, he would, probably, have distinguished himself in those branches of literature which call for taste and imagination, rather than any exertion of reflection or judgment. As it was, his literary taste showed itself in making collections of Cambrian antiquities of every description, till his stock of Welsh MSS. would have excited the envy of Dr. Pugh himself, had he been alive at the time of which I write.

There is one characteristic of Robert Griffiths which I have omitted to note, and which was peculiar among his class. He was no hard drinker; whether it was that his head was easily affected, or that his partially-refined taste led him to dislike intoxication and its attendant circumstances, I cannot say; but at five-and-twenty Robert Griffiths was habitually sober—a thing so rare in Llyn, that he was almost shunned as a churlish, unsociable being, and paused much of his time in solitude.

About this time, he had to appear in some case that was tried at the Caernarvon assizes; and while there, was a guest at the house of his agent, a shrewd, sensible Welsh attorney, with one daughter, who had charms enough to captivate Robert Griffiths. Though he remained only a few days at her father's house, they were sufficient to decide his affections, and short was the period allowed to elapse before he brought home a mistress to Bodowen. The new Mrs. Griffiths was a gentle, yielding person, full of love toward her husband, of whom, nevertheless, she stood something in awe, partly arising from the difference in their ages, partly from his devoting much time to studies of which she could understand nothing.

She soon made him the father of a blooming little daughter, called Augharad after her mother. Then there came several uneventful years in the household of Bodowen; and when the old women had one and all declared that the cradle would not rock again, Mrs. Griffiths bore the son and heir. His birth was soon followed by his mother's death: she had been ailing and low-spirited during her pregnancy, and she seemed to lack the buoyancy of body and mind requisite to bring her round after her time of trial. Her husband, who loved her all the more from having few other claims on his affections, was deeply grieved by her early death, and his only comforter was the sweet little boy whom she had left behind. That part of the squire's character, which was so tender, and almost feminine, seemed called forth by the helpless situation of the little infant, who stretched out his arms to his father with the same earnest cooing that happier children make use of to their mother alone. Augharad was almost neglected, while the little Owen was king of the house; still next to his father, none tended him so lovingly as his sister. She was so accustomed to give way to him that it was no longer a hardship. By night and by day Owen was the constant companion of his father, and increasing years seemed only to confirm the custom. It was an unnatural life for the child, seeing no bright little faces peering into his own (for Augharad was, as I said before, five or six years older, and her face, poor motherless girl! was often anything but bright), hearing no din of clear ringing voices, but day after day sharing the otherwise solitary hours of his father, whether in the dim room, surrounded by wizard-like antiquities, or pattering his little feet to keep up with his "tada" in his mountain rambles or shooting excursions. When the pair came to some little foaming brook, where the stepping-stones were far and wide, the father carried his little boy across with the tenderest care; when the lad was weary, they rested, he cradled in his father's arms, or the Squire would lift him up and carry him to his home again. The boy was indulged (for his father felt flattered by the desire) in his wish of sharing his meals and keeping the same hours. All this indulgence did not render Owen unamiable, but it made him wilful, and not a happy child. He had a thoughtful look, not common to the face of a young boy. He knew no games, no merry sports; his information was of an imaginative and speculative character. His father delighted to interest him in his own studies, without considering how far they were healthy for so young a mind.

Of course Squire Griffiths was not unaware of the prophecy which was to be fulfilled in his generation. He would occasionally refer to it when among his friends, with sceptical levity; but in truth it lay nearer to his heart than he chose to acknowledge. His strong imagination rendered him peculiarly impressible on such subjects; while his judgment, seldom exercised or fortified by severe thought, could not prevent his continually recurring to it. He used to gaze on the half-sad countenance of the child, who sat looking up into his face with his large dark eyes, so fondly yet so inquiringly, till the old legend swelled around his heart, and became too painful for him not to require sympathy. Besides, the overpowering love he bore to the child seemed to demand fuller vent than tender words; it made him like, yet dread, to upbraid its object for the fearful contrast foretold. Still Squire Griffiths told the legend, in a half-jesting manner, to his little son, when they were roaming over the wild heaths in the autumn days, "the saddest of the year," or while they sat in the oak-wainscoted room, surrounded by mysterious relics that gleamed strangely forth by the flickering fire-light. The legend was wrought into the boy's mind, and he would crave, yet tremble, to hear it told over and over again, while the words were intermingled with caresses and questions as to his love. Occasionally his loving words and actions were cut short by his father's light yet bitter speech—"Get thee away, my lad; thou knowest not what is to come of all this love."

When Augharad was seventeen, and Owen eleven or twelve, the rector of the parish in which Bodowen was situated, endeavoured to prevail on Squire Griffiths to send the boy to school. Now, this rector had many congenial tastes with his parishioner, and was his only intimate; and, by repeated arguments, he succeeded in convincing the Squire that the unnatural life Owen was leading was in every way injurious. Unwillingly was the father wrought to part from his son; but he did at length send him to the Grammar School at Bangor, then under the management of an excellent classic. Here Owen showed that he had more talents than the rector had given him credit for, when he affirmed that the lad had been completely stupefied by the life he led at Bodowen. He bade fair to do credit to the school in the peculiar branch of learning for which it was famous. But he was not popular among his schoolfellows. He was wayward, though, to a certain degree, generous and unselfish; he was reserved but gentle, except when the tremendous bursts of passion (similar in character to those of his father) forced their way.

On his return from school one Christmas-time, when he had been a year or so at Bangor, he was stunned by hearing that the undervalued Augharad was about to be married to a gentleman of South Wales, residing near Aberystwith. Boys seldom appreciate their sisters; but Owen thought of the many slights with which he had requited the patient Augharad, and he gave way to bitter regrets, which, with a selfish want of control over his words, he kept expressing to his father, until the Squire was thoroughly hurt and chagrined at the repeated exclamations of "What shall we do when Augharad is gone?" "How dull we shall be when Augharad is married!" Owen's holidays were prolonged a few weeks, in order that he might be present at the wedding; and when all the festivities were over, and the bride and bridegroom had left Bodowen, the boy and his father really felt how much they missed the quiet, loving Augharad. She had performed so many thoughtful, noiseless little offices, on which their daily comfort depended; and now she was gone, the household seemed to miss the spirit that peacefully kept it in order; the servants roamed about in search of commands and directions, the rooms had no longer the unobtrusive ordering of taste to make them cheerful, the very fires burned dim, and were always sinking down into dull heaps of gray ashes. Altogether Owen did not regret his return to Bangor, and this also the mortified parent perceived. Squire Griffiths was a selfish parent.

Letters in those days were a rare occurrence. Owen usually received one during his half-yearly absences from home, and occasionally his father paid him a visit. This half-year the boy had no visit, nor even a letter, till very near the time of his leaving school, and then he was astounded by the intelligence that his father was married again.

Then came one of his paroxysms of rage; the more disastrous in its effects upon his character because it could find no vent in action. Independently of slight to the memory of the first wife which children are so apt to fancy such an action implies, Owen had hitherto considered himself (and with justice) the first object of his father's life. They had been so much to each other; and now a shapeless, but too real something had come between him and his father there for ever. He felt as if his permission should have been asked, as if he should have been consulted. Certainly he ought to have been told of the intended event. So the Squire felt, and hence his constrained letter which had so much increased the bitterness of Owen's feelings.

With all this anger, when Owen saw his stepmother, he thought he had never seen so beautiful a woman for her age; for she was no longer in the bloom of youth, being a widow when his father married her. Her manners, to the Welsh lad, who had seen little of female grace among the families of the few antiquarians with whom his father visited, were so fascinating that he watched her with a sort of breathless admiration. Her measured grace, her faultless movements, her tones of voice, sweet, till the ear was sated with their sweetness, made Owen less angry at his father's marriage. Yet he felt, more than ever, that the cloud was between him and his father; that the hasty letter he had sent in answer to the announcement of his wedding was not forgotten, although no allusion was ever made to it. He was no longer his father's confidant—hardly ever his father's companion, for the newly-married wife was all in all to the Squire, and his son felt himself almost a cipher, where he had so long been everything. The lady herself had ever the softest consideration for her stepson; almost too obtrusive was the attention paid to his wishes, but still he fancied that the heart had no part in the winning advances. There was a watchful glance of the eye that Owen once or twice caught when she had imagined herself unobserved, and many other nameless little circumstances, that gave him a strong feeling of want of sincerity in his stepmother. Mrs. Owen brought with her into the family her little child by her first husband, a boy nearly three years old. He was one of those elfish, observant, mocking children, over whose feelings you seem to have no control: agile and mischievous, his little practical jokes, at first performed in ignorance of the pain he gave, but afterward proceeding to a malicious pleasure in suffering, really seemed to afford some ground to the superstitious notion of some of the common people that he was a fairy changeling.

Years passed on; and as Owen grew older he became more observant. He saw, even in his occasional visits at home (for from school he had passed on to college), that a great change had taken place in the outward manifestations of his father's character; and, by degrees, Owen traced this change to the influence of his stepmother; so slight, so imperceptible to the common observer, yet so resistless in its effects. Squire Griffiths caught up his wife's humbly advanced opinions, and, unawares to himself, adopted them as his own, defying all argument and opposition. It was the same with her wishes; they met their fulfilment, from the extreme and delicate art with which she insinuated them into her husband's mind, as his own. She sacrificed the show of authority for the power. At last, when Owen perceived some oppressive act in his father's conduct toward his dependants, or some unaccountable thwarting of his own wishes, he fancied he saw his stepmother's secret influence thus displayed, however much she might regret the injustice of his father's actions in her conversations with him when they were alone. His father was fast losing his temperate habits, and frequent intoxication soon took its usual effect upon the temper. Yet even here was the spell of his wife upon him. Before her he placed a restraint upon his passion, yet she was perfectly aware of his irritable disposition, and directed it hither and thither with the same apparent ignorance of the tendency of her words.

Meanwhile Owen's situation became peculiarly mortifying to a youth whose early remembrances afforded such a contrast to his present state. As a child, he had been elevated to the consequence of a man before his years gave any mental check to the selfishness which such conduct was likely to engender; he could remember when his will was law to the servants and dependants, and his sympathy necessary to his father: now he was as a cipher in his father's house; and the Squire, estranged in the first instance by a feeling of the injury he had done his son in not sooner acquainting him with his purposed marriage, seemed rather to avoid than to seek him as a companion, and too frequently showed the most utter indifference to the feelings and wishes which a young man of a high and independent spirit might be supposed to indulge.

Perhaps Owen was not fully aware of the force of all these circumstances; for an actor in a family drama is seldom unimpassioned enough to be perfectly observant. But he became moody and soured; brooding over his unloved existence, and craving with a human heart after sympathy.

This feeling took more full possession of his mind when he had left college, and returned home to lead an idle and purposeless life. As the heir, there was no worldly necessity for exertion: his father was too much of a Welsh squire to dream of the moral necessity, and he himself had not sufficient strength of mind to decide at once upon abandoning a place and mode of life which abounded in daily mortifications; yet to this course his judgment was slowly tending, when some circumstances occurred to detain him at Bodowen.

It was not to be expected that harmony would long be preserved, even in appearance, between an unguarded and soured young man, such as Owen, and his wary stepmother, when he had once left college, and come, not as a visitor, but as the heir to his father's house. Some cause of difference occurred, where the woman subdued her hidden anger sufficiently to become convinced that Owen was not entirely the dupe she had believed him to be. Henceforward there was no peace between them. Not in vulgar altercations did this show itself; but in moody reserve on Owen's part, and in undisguised and contemptuous pursuance of her own plans by his father. Bodowen was no longer a place where, if Owen was not loved or attended to, he could at least find peace, and care for himself: he was thwarted at every step, and in every wish, by his father's desire, apparently, while the wife sat by with a smile of triumph on her beautiful lips.

So Owen went forth at the early day dawn, sometimes roaming about on the shore or the upland, shooting or fishing, as the season might be, but oftener "stretched in indolent repose" on the short, sweet grass, indulging in gloomy and morbid reveries. He would fancy that this mortified state of existence was a dream, a horrible dream, from which he should awake and find himself again the sole object and darling of his father. And then he would start up and strive to shake off the incubus. There was the molten sunset of his childish memory; the gorgeous crimson piles of glory in the west, fading away into the cold calm light of the rising moon, while here and there a cloud floated across the western heaven, like a seraph's wing, in its flaming beauty; the earth was the same as in his childhood's days, full of gentle evening sounds, and the harmonies of twilight—the breeze came sweeping low over the heather and blue-bells by his side, and the turf was sending up its evening incense of perfume. But life, and heart, and hope were changed for ever since those bygone days!

Or he would seat himself in a favourite niche of the rocks on Moel Gêst, hidden by a stunted growth of the whitty, or mountain-ash, from general observation, with a rich-tinted cushion of stone-crop for his feet, and a straight precipice of rock rising just above. Here would he sit for hours, gazing idly at the bay below with its back-ground of purple hills, and the little fishing-sail on its bosom, showing white in the sunbeam, and gliding on in such harmony with the quiet beauty of the glassy sea; or he would pull out an old school-volume, his companion for years, and in morbid accordance with the dark legend that still lurked in the recesses of his mind—a shape of gloom in those innermost haunts awaiting its time to come forth in distinct outline—would he turn to the old Greek dramas which treat of a family foredoomed by an avenging Fate. The worn page opened of itself at the play of the Œdipus Tyrannus, and Owen dwelt with the craving disease upon the prophecy so nearly resembling that which concerned himself. With his consciousness of neglect, there was a sort of self-flattery in the consequence which the legend gave him. He almost wondered how they durst, with slights and insults, thus provoke the Avenger.

The days drifted onward. Often he would vehemently pursue some sylvan sport, till thought and feeling were lost in the violence of bodily exertion. Occasionally his evenings were spent at a small public-house, such as stood by the unfrequented wayside, where the welcome, hearty, though bought, seemed so strongly to contrast with the gloomy negligence of home—unsympathising home.

One evening (Owen might be four or five-and-twenty), wearied with a day's shooting on the Clenneny Moors, he passed by the open door of "The Goat" at Penmorfa. The light and the cheeriness within tempted him, poor self-exhausted man! as it has done many a one more wretched in worldly circumstances, to step in, and take his evening meal where at least his presence was of some consequence. It was a busy day in that little hostel. A flock of sheep, amounting to some hundreds, had arrived at Penmorfa, on their road to England, and thronged the space before the house. Inside was the shrewd, kind-hearted hostess, bustling to and fro, with merry greetings for every tired drover who was to pass the night in her house, while the sheep were penned in a field close by. Ever and anon, she kept attending to the second crowd of guests, who were celebrating a rural wedding in her house. It was busy work to Martha Thomas, yet her smile never flagged; and when Owen Griffiths had finished his evening meal she was there, ready with a hope that it had done him good, and was to his mind, and a word of intelligence that the wedding-folk were about to dance in the kitchen, and the harper was the famous Edward of Corwen.

Owen, partly from good-natured compliance with his hostess's implied wish, and partly from curiosity, lounged to the passage which led to the kitchen—not the every-day, working, cooking kitchen, which was behind, but a good-sized room, where the mistress sat, when her work was done, and where the country people were commonly entertained at such merry-makings as the present. The lintels of the door formed a frame for the animated picture which Owen saw within, as he leaned against the wall in the dark passage. The red light of the fire, with every now and then a falling piece of turf sending forth a fresh blaze, shone full upon four young men who were dancing a measure something like a Scotch reel, keeping admirable time in their rapid movements to the capital tune the harper was playing. They had their hats on when Owen first took his stand, but as they grew more and more animated they flung them away, and presently their shoes were kicked off with like disregard to the spot where they might happen to alight. Shouts of applause followed any remarkable exertion of agility, in which each seemed to try to excel his companions. At length, wearied and exhausted, they sat down, and the harper gradually changed to one of those wild, inspiring national airs for which he was so famous. The thronged audience sat earnest and breathless, and you might have heard a pin drop, except when some maiden passed hurriedly, with flaring candle and busy look, through to the real kitchen beyond. When he had finished his beautiful theme on "The March of the men of Harlech," he changed the measure again to "Tri chant o' bunnan" (Three hundred pounds), and immediately a most unmusical-looking man began chanting "Pennillion," or a sort of recitative stanzas, which were soon taken up by another, and this amusement lasted so long that Owen grew weary, and was thinking of retreating from his post by the door, when some little bustle was occasioned, on the opposite side of the room, by the entrance of a middle-aged man, and a young girl, apparently his daughter. The man advanced to the bench occupied by the seniors of the party, who welcomed him with the usual pretty Welsh greeting, "Pa sut mae dy galon?" ("How is thy heart?") and drinking his health passed on to him the cup of excellent cwrw. The girl, evidently a village belle, was as warmly greeted by the young men, while the girls eyed her rather askance with a half-jealous look, which Owen set down to the score of her extreme prettiness. Like most Welsh women, she was of middle size as to height, but beautifully made, with the most perfect yet delicate roundness in every limb. Her little mob-cap was carefully adjusted to a face which was excessively pretty, though it never could be called handsome. It also was round, with the slightest tendency to the oval shape, richly coloured, though somewhat olive in complexion, with dimples in cheek and chin, and the most scarlet lips Owen had ever seen, that were too short to meet over the small pearly teeth. The nose was the most defective feature; but the eyes were splendid. They were so long, so lustrous, yet at times so very soft under their thick fringe of eyelash! The nut-brown hair was carefully braided beneath the border of delicate lace: it was evident the little village beauty knew how to make the most of all her attractions, for the gay colours which were displayed in her neckerchief were in complete harmony with the complexion.

Owen was much attracted, while yet he was amused, by the evident coquetry the girl displayed, collecting around her a whole bevy of young fellows, for each of whom she seemed to have some gay speech, some attractive look or action. In a few minutes young Griffiths of Bodowen was at her side, brought thither by a variety of idle motives, and as her undivided attention was given to the Welsh heir, her admirers, one by one, dropped off, to seat themselves by some less fascinating but more attentive fair one. The more Owen conversed with the girl, the more he was taken; she had more wit and talent than he had fancied possible; a self-abandon and thoughtfulness, to boot, that seemed full of charms; and then her voice was so clear and sweet, and her actions so full of grace, that Owen was fascinated before he was well aware, and kept looking into her bright, blushing face, till her uplifted flashing eye fell beneath his earnest gaze.

While it thus happened that they were silent—she from confusion at the unexpected warmth of his admiration, he from an unconsciousness of anything but the beautiful changes in her flexile countenance—the man whom Owen took for her father came up and addressed some observation to his daughter, from whence he glided into some commonplace though respectful remark to Owen, and at length engaging him in some slight, local conversation, he led the way to the account of a spot on the peninsula of Penthryn, where teal abounded, and concluded with begging Owen to allow him to show him the exact place, saying that whenever the young Squire felt so inclined, if he would honour him by a call at his house, he would take him across in his boat. While Owen listened, his attention was not so much absorbed as to be unaware that the little beauty at his side was refusing one or two who endeavoured to draw her from her place by invitations to dance. Flattered by his own construction of her refusals, he again directed all his attention to her, till she was called away by her father, who was leaving the scene of festivity. Before he left he reminded Owen of his promise, and added—

"Perhaps, sir, you do not know me. My name is Ellis Pritchard, and I live at Ty Glas, on this side of Moel Gêst; anyone can point it out to you."

When the father and daughter had left, Owen slowly prepared for his ride home; but encountering the hostess, he could not resist asking a few questions relative to Ellis Pritchard and his pretty daughter. She answered shortly but respectfully, and then said, rather hesitatingly—

"Master Griffiths, you know the triad, 'Tri pheth tebyg y naill i'r llall, ysgnbwr heb yd, mail deg heb ddiawd, a merch deg heb ei geirda' (Three things are alike: a fine barn without corn, a fine cup without drink, a fine woman without her reputation)." She hastily quitted him, and Owen rode slowly to his unhappy home.

Ellis Pritchard, half farmer and half fisherman, was shrewd, and keen, and worldly; yet he was good-natured, and sufficiently generous to have become rather a popular man among his equals. He had been struck with the young Squire's attention to his pretty daughter, and was not insensible to the advantages to be derived from it. Nest would not be the first peasant girl, by any means, who had been transplanted to a Welsh manor-house as its mistress; and, accordingly, her father had shrewdly given the admiring young man some pretext for further opportunities of seeing her.

As for Nest herself, she had somewhat of her father's worldliness, and was fully alive to the superior station of her new admirer, and quite prepared to slight all her old sweethearts on his account. But then she had something more of feeling in her reckoning; she had not been insensible to the earnest yet comparatively refined homage which Owen paid her; she had noticed his expressive and occasionally handsome countenance with admiration, and was flattered by his so immediately singling her out from her companions. As to the hint which Martha Thomas had thrown out, it is enough to say that Nest was very giddy, and that she was motherless. She had high spirits and a great love of admiration, or, to use a softer term, she loved to please; men, women, and children, all, she delighted to gladden with her smile and voice. She coquetted, and flirted, and went to the extreme lengths of Welsh courtship, till the seniors of the village shook their heads, and cautioned their daughters against her acquaintance. If not absolutely guilty, she had too frequently been on the verge of guilt.

Even at the time, Martha Thomas's hint made but little impression on Owen, for his senses were otherwise occupied; but in a few days the recollection thereof had wholly died away, and one warm glorious summer's day, he bent his steps toward Ellis Pritchard's with a beating heart; for, except some very slight flirtations at Oxford, Owen had never been touched; his thoughts, his fancy, had been otherwise engaged.

Ty Glas was built against one of the lower rocks of Moel Gêst, which, indeed, formed a side to the low, lengthy house. The materials of the cottage were the shingly stones which had fallen from above, plastered rudely together, with deep recesses for the small oblong windows. Altogether, the exterior was much ruder than Owen had expected; but inside there seemed no lack of comforts. The house was divided into two apartments, one large, roomy, and dark, into which Owen entered immediately; and before the blushing Nest came from the inner chamber (for she had seen the young Squire coming, and hastily gone to make some alteration in her dress), he had had time to look around him, and note the various little particulars of the room. Beneath the window (which commanded a magnificent view) was an oaken dresser, replete with drawers and cupboards, and brightly polished to a rich dark colour. In the farther part of the room Owen could at first distinguish little, entering as he did from the glaring sunlight, but he soon saw that there were two oaken beds, closed up after the manner of the Welsh: in fact, the domitories of Ellis Pritchard and the man who served under him, both on sea and on land. There was the large wheel used for spinning wool, left standing on the middle of the floor, as if in use only a few minutes before; and around the ample chimney hung flitches of bacon, dried kids'-flesh, and fish, that was in process of smoking for winter's store.

Before Nest had shyly dared to enter, her father, who had been mending his nets down below, and seen Owen winding up to the house, came in and gave him a hearty yet respectful welcome; and then Nest, downcast and blushing, full of the consciousness which her father's advice and conversation had not failed to inspire, ventured to join them. To Owen's mind this reserve and shyness gave her new charms.

It was too bright, too hot, too anything to think of going to shoot teal till later in the day, and Owen was delighted to accept a hesitating invitation to share the noonday meal. Some ewe-milk cheese, very hard and dry, oat-cake, slips of the dried kids'-flesh broiled, after having been previously soaked in water for a few minutes, delicious butter and fresh butter-milk, with a liquor called "diod griafol" (made from the berries of the Sorbus aucuparia, infused in water and then fermented), composed the frugal repast; but there was something so clean and neat, and withal such a true welcome, that Owen had seldom enjoyed a meal so much. Indeed, at that time of day the Welsh squires differed from the farmers more in the plenty and rough abundance of their manner of living than in the refinement of style of their table.

At the present day, down in Llyn, the Welsh gentry are not a wit behind their Saxon equals in the expensive elegances of life; but then (when there was but one pewter-service in all Northumberland) there was nothing in Ellis Pritchard's mode of living that grated on the young Squire's sense of refinement.

Little was said by that young pair of wooers during the meal; the father had all the conversation to himself, apparently heedless of the ardent looks and inattentive mien of his guest. As Owen became more serious in his feelings, he grew more timid in their expression, and at night, when they returned from their shooting-excursion, the caress he gave Nest was almost as bashfully offered as received.

This was but the first of a series of days devoted to Nest in reality, though at first he thought some little disguise of his object was necessary. The past, the future, was all forgotten in those happy days of love.

And every worldly plan, every womanly wile was put in practice by Ellis Pritchard and his daughter, to render his visits agreeable and alluring. Indeed, the very circumstance of his being welcome was enough to attract the poor young man, to whom the feeling so produced was new and full of charms. He left a home where the certainty of being thwarted made him chary in expressing his wishes; where no tones of love ever fell on his ear, save those addressed to others; where his presence or absence was a matter of utter indifference; and when he entered Ty Glas, all, down to the little cur which, with clamorous barkings, claimed a part of his attention, seemed to rejoice. His account of his day's employment found a willing listener in Ellis; and when he passed on to Nest, busy at her wheel or at her churn, the deepened colour, the conscious eye, and the gradual yielding of herself up to his lover-like caress, had worlds of charms. Ellis Pritchard was a tenant on the Bodowen estate, and therefore had reasons in plenty for wishing to keep the young Squire's visits secret; and Owen, unwilling to disturb the sunny calm of these halcyon days by any storm at home, was ready to use all the artifice which Ellis suggested as to the mode of his calls at Ty Glas. Nor was he unaware of the probable, nay, the hoped-for termination of these repeated days of happiness. He was quite conscious that the father wished for nothing better than the marriage of his daughter to the heir of Bodowen; and when Nest had hidden her face in his neck, which was encircled by her clasping arms, and murmured into his ear her acknowledgment of love, he felt only too desirous of finding some one to love him for ever. Though not highly principled, he would not have tried to obtain Nest on other terms save those of marriage: he did so pine after enduring love, and fancied he should have bound her heart for evermore to his, when they had taken the solemn oaths of matrimony.

There was no great difficulty attending a secret marriage at such a place and at such a time. One gusty autumn day, Ellis ferried them round Penthryn to Llandutrwyn, and there saw his little Nest become future Lady of Bodowen.

How often do we see giddy, coquetting, restless girls become sobered by marriage? A great object in life is decided; one on which their thoughts have been running in all their vagaries, and they seem to verify the beautiful fable of Undine. A new soul beams out in the gentleness and repose of their future lives. An indescribable softness and tenderness takes place of the wearying vanity of their former endeavours to attract admiration. Something of this sort took place in Nest Pritchard. If at first she had been anxious to attract the young Squire of Bodowen, long before her marriage this feeling had merged into a truer love than she had ever felt before; and now that he was her own, her husband, her whole soul was bent toward making him amends, as far as in her lay, for the misery which, with a woman's tact, she saw that he had to endure at his home. Her greetings were abounding in delicately-expressed love; her study of his tastes unwearying, in the arrangement of her dress, her time, her very thoughts.

No wonder that he looked back on his wedding-day with a thankfulness which is seldom the result of unequal marriages. No wonder that his heart beat aloud as formerly when he wound up the little path to Ty Glas, and saw—keen though the winter's wind might be—that Nest was standing out at the door to watch for his dimly-seen approach, while the candle flared in the little window as a beacon to guide him aright.

The angry words and unkind actions of home fell deadened on his heart; he thought of the love that was surely his, and of the new promise of love that a short time would bring forth, and he could almost have smiled at the impotent efforts to disturb his peace.

A few more months, and the young father was greeted by a feeble little cry, when he hastily entered Ty Glas, one morning early, in consequence of a summons conveyed mysteriously to Bodowen; and the pale mother, smiling, and feebly holding up her babe to its father's kiss, seemed to him even more lovely than the bright gay Nest who had won his heart at the little inn of Penmorfa.

But the curse was at work! The fulfilment of the prophecy was nigh at hand!

CHAPTER II

IT was the autumn after the birth of their boy; it had been a glorious summer, with bright, hot, sunny weather; and now the year was fading away as seasonably into mellow days, with mornings of silver mists and clear frosty nights. The blooming look of the time of flowers, was past and gone; but instead there were even richer tints abroad in the sun-coloured leaves, the lichens, the golden blossomed furze; if it was the time of fading, there was a glory in the decay.

Nest, in her loving anxiety to surround her dwelling with every charm for her husband's sake, had turned gardener, and the little corners of the rude court before the house were filled with many a delicate mountain-flower, transplanted more for its beauty than its rarity. The sweetbrier bush may even yet be seen, old and gray, which she and Owen planted a green slipling beneath the window of her little chamber. In those moments Owen forgot all besides the present; all the cares and griefs he had known in the past, and all that might await him of woe and death in the future. The boy, too, was as lovely a child as the fondest parent was ever blessed with; and crowed with delight, and clapped his little hands, as his mother held him in her arms at the cottage-door to watch his father's ascent up the rough path that led to Ty Glas, one bright autumnal morning; and when the three entered the house together, it was difficult to say which was the happiest. Owen carried his boy, and tossed and played with him, while Nest sought out some little article of work, and seated herself on the dresser beneath the window, where now busily plying the needle, and then again looking at her husband, she eagerly told him the little pieces of domestic intelligence, the winning ways of the child, the result of yesterday's fishing, and such of the gossip of Penmorfa as came to the ears of the now retired Nest. She noticed that, when she mentioned any little circumstance which bore the slightest reference to Bodowen, her husband appeared chafed and uneasy, and at last avoided anything that might in the least remind him of home. In truth, he had been suffering much of late from the irritability of his father, shown in trifles to be sure, but not the less galling on that account.

While they were thus talking, and caressing each other and the child, a shadow darkened the room, and before they could catch a glimpse of the object that had occasioned it, it vanished, and Squire Griffiths lifted the door-latch and stood before them. He stood and looked—first on his son, so different, in his buoyant expression of content and enjoyment, with his noble child in his arms, like a proud and happy father, as he was, from the depressed, moody young man he too often appeared at Bodowen; then on Nest—poor, trembling, sickened Nest!—who dropped her work, but yet durst not stir from her seat, on the dresser, while she looked to her husband as if for protection from his father.

The Squire was silent, as he glared from one to the other, his features white with restrained passion. When he spoke, his words came most distinct in their forced composure. It was to his son he addressed himself:

"That woman! who is she?"

Owen hesitated one moment, and then replied, in a steady, yet quiet voice:

"Father, that woman is my wife."

He would have added some apology for the long concealment of his marriage; have appealed to his father's forgiveness; but the foam flew from Squire Owen's lips as he burst forth with invective against Nest:—

"You have married her! It is as they told me! Married Nest Pritchard yr buten! And you stand there as if you had not disgraced yourself for ever and ever with your accursed wiving! And the fair harlot sits there, in her mocking modesty, practising the mimming airs that will become her state as future Lady of Bodowen. But I will move heaven and earth before that false woman darken the doors of my father's house as mistress!"

All this was said with such rapidity that Owen had no time for the words that thronged to his lips. "Father!" (he burst forth at length) "Father, whosoever told you that Nest Pritchard was a harlot told you a lie as false as hell! Ay! a lie as false as hell!" he added, in a voice of thunder, while he advanced a step or two nearer to the Squire. And then, in a lower tone, he said—

"She is as pure as your own wife; nay, God help me! as the dear, precious mother who brought me forth, and then left me—with no refuge in a mother's heart—to struggle on through life alone. I tell you Nest is as pure as that dear, dead mother!"

"Fool—poor fool!"

At this moment the child—the little Owen—who had kept gazing from one angry countenance to the other, and with earnest look, trying to understand what had brought the fierce glare into the face where till now he had read nothing but love, in some way attracted the Squire's attention, and increased his wrath.

"Yes," he continued, "poor, weak fool that you are, hugging the child of another as if it were your own offspring!" Owen involuntarily caressed the affrighted child, and half smiled at the implication of his father's words. This the Squire perceived, and raising his voice to a scream of rage, he went on:

"I bid you, if you call yourself my son, to cast away that miserable, shameless woman's offspring; cast it away this instant—this instant!"

In this ungovernable rage, seeing that Owen was far from complying with his command, he snatched the poor infant from the loving arms that held it, and throwing it to his mother, left the house inarticulate with fury.

Nest—who had been pale and still as marble during this terrible dialogue, looking on and listening as if fascinated by the words that smote her heart—opened her arms to receive and cherish her precious babe; but the boy was not destined to reach the white refuge of her breast. The furious action of the

Squire had been almost without aim, and the infant fell against the sharp edge of the dresser down on to the stone floor.

Owen sprang up to take the child, but he lay so still, so motionless, that the awe of death came over the father, and he stooped down to gaze more closely. At that moment, the upturned, filmy eyes rolled convulsively—a spasm passed along the body—and the lips, yet warm with kissing, quivered into everlasting rest.

A word from her husband told Nest all. She slid down from her seat, and lay by her little son as corpse-like as he, unheeding all the agonizing endearments and passionate adjurations of her husband. And that poor, desolate husband and father! Scarce one little quarter of an hour, and he had been so blessed in his consciousness of love! the bright promise of many years on his infant's face, and the new, fresh soul beaming forth in its awakened intelligence. And there it was; the little clay image, that would never more gladden up at the sight of him, nor stretch forth to meet his embrace; whose inarticulate, yet most eloquent cooings might haunt him in his dreams, but would never more be heard in waking life again! And by the dead babe, almost as utterly insensate, the poor mother had fallen in a merciful faint—the slandered, heart-pierced Nest! Owen struggled against the sickness that came over him, and busied himself in vain attempts at her restoration.

It was now near noon-day, and Ellis Pritchard came home, little dreaming of the sight that awaited him; but though stunned, he was able to take more effectual measures for his poor daughter's recovery than Owen had done.

By-and-by she showed symptoms of returning sense, and was placed in her own little bed in a darkened room, where, without ever waking to complete consciousness, she fell asleep. Then it was that her husband, suffocated by pressure of miserable thought, gently drew his hand from her tightened clasp, and printing one long soft kiss on her white waxen forehead, hastily stole out of the room, and out of the house.

Near the base of Moel Gêst—it might be a quarter of a mile from Ty Glas—was a little neglected solitary copse, wild and tangled with the trailing branches of the dog-rose and the tendrils of the white bryony. Toward the middle of this thicket a deep crystal pool—a clear mirror for the blue heavens above—and round the margin floated the broad green leaves of the water-lily, and when the regal sun shone down in his noonday glory the flowers arose from their cool depths to welcome and greet him. The copse was musical with many sounds; the warbling of birds rejoicing in its shades, the ceaseless hum of the insects that hovered over the pool, the chime of the distant waterfall, the occasional bleating of the sheep from the mountaintop, were all blended into the delicious harmony of nature.

It had been one of Owen's favourite resorts when he had been a lonely wanderer—a pilgrim in search of love in the years gone by. And thither he went, as if by instinct, when he left Ty Glas; quelling the uprising agony till he should reach that little solitary spot.

It was the time of day when a change in the aspect of the weather so frequently takes place; and the little pool was no longer the reflection of a blue and sunny sky: it sent back the dark and slaty clouds above, and, every now and then, a rough gust shook the painted autumn leaves from their branches, and all other music was lost in the sound of the wild winds piping down from the moorlands, which lay up and beyond the clefts in the mountain-side. Presently the rain came on and beat down in torrents.

But Owen heeded it not. He sat on the dank ground, his face buried in his hands, and his whole strength, physical and mental, employed in quelling the rush of blood, which rose and boiled and gurgled in his brain as if it would madden him.

The phantom of his dead child rose ever before him, and seemed to cry aloud for vengeance. And when the poor young man thought upon the victim whom he required in his wild longing for revenge, he shuddered, for it was his father!

Again and again he tried not to think; but still the circle of thought came round, eddying through his brain. At length he mastered his passions, and they were calm; then he forced himself to arrange some plan for the future.

He had not, in the passionate hurry of the moment, seen that his father had left the cottage before he was aware of the fatal accident that befell the child. Owen thought he had seen all; and once he planned to go to the Squire and tell him of the anguish of heart he had wrought, and awe him, as it were, by the dignity of grief. But then again he durst not—he distrusted his self-control—the old prophecy rose up in its horror—he dreaded his doom.

At last he determined to leave his father for ever; to take Nest to some distant country where she might forget her firstborn, and where he himself might gain a livelihood by his own exertions.

But when he tried to descend to the various little arrangements which were involved in the execution of this plan, he remembered that all his money (and in this respect Squire Griffiths was no niggard) was locked up in his escritoire at Bodowen. In vain he tried to do away with this matter-of-fact difficulty; go to Bodowen he must: and his only hope—nay his determination—was to avoid his father.

He rose and took a by-path to Bodowen. The house looked even more gloomy and desolate than usual in the heavy down-pouring rain, yet Owen gazed on it with something of regret—for sorrowful as his days in it had been, he was about to leave it for many many years, if not for ever. He entered by a side door opening into a passage that led to his own room, where he kept his books, his guns, his fishing-tackle, his writing materials, et cetera.

Here he hurriedly began to select the few articles he intended to take; for, besides the dread of interruption, he was feverishly anxious to travel far that very night, if only Nest was capable of performing the journey. As he was thus employed, he tried to conjecture what his father's feelings would be on finding that his once-loved son was gone away for ever. Would he then awaken to regret for the conduct which had driven him from home, and bitterly think on the loving and caressing boy who haunted his footsteps in former days? Or, alas! would he only feel that an obstacle to his daily happiness—to his contentment with his wife, and his strange, doting affection for the child—was taken away? Would they make merry over the heir's departure? Then he thought of Nest—the young childless mother, whose heart had not yet realized her fulness of desolation. Poor Nest! so loving as she was, so devoted to her child—how should he console her? He pictured her away in a strange land, pining for her native mountains, and refusing to be comforted because her child was not.

Even this thought of the home-sickness that might possibly beset Nest hardly made him hesitate in his determination; so strongly had the idea taken possession of him that only by putting miles and leagues between him and his father could he avert the doom which seemed blending itself with the very purposes of his life as long as he stayed in proximity with the slayer of his child.

He had now nearly completed his hasty work of preparation, and was full of tender thoughts of his wife, when the door opened, and the elfish Robert peered in, in search of some of his brother's possessions. On seeing Owen he hesitated, but then came boldly forward, and laid his hand on Owen's arm, saying,

"Nesta yr buten! How is Nest yr buten?"

He looked maliciously into Owen's face to mark the effect of his words, but was terrified at the expression he read there. He started off and ran to the door, while Owen tried to check himself, saying continually, "He is but a child. He does not understand the meaning of what he says. He is but a child!" Still Robert, now in fancied security, kept calling out his insulting words, and Owen's hand was on his gun, grasping it as if to restrain his rising fury.

But when Robert passed on daringly to mocking words relating to the poor dead child, Owen could bear it no longer; and before the boy was well aware, Owen was fiercely holding him in an iron clasp with one hand, while he struck him hard with the other.

In a minute he checked himself. He paused, relaxed his grasp, and, to his horror, he saw Robert sink to the ground; in fact, the lad was half-stunned, half-frightened, and thought it best to assume insensibility.

Owen—miserable Owen—seeing him lie there prostrate, was bitterly repentant, and would have dragged him to the carved settle, and done all he could to restore him to his senses, but at this instant the Squire came in.

Probably, when the household at Bodowen rose that morning, there was but one among them ignorant of the heir's relation to Nest Pritchard and her child; for secret as he tried to make his visits to Ty Glas, they had been too frequent not to be noticed, and Nest's altered conduct—no longer frequenting dances and merry-makings—was a strongly corroborative circumstance. But Mrs. Griffiths' influence reigned paramount, if unacknowledged, at Bodowen, and till she sanctioned the disclosure, none would dare to tell the Squire.

Now, however, the time drew near when it suited her to make her husband aware of the connection his son had formed; so, with many tears, and much seeming reluctance, she broke the intelligence to him— taking good care, at the same time, to inform him of the light character Nest had borne. Nor did she confine this evil reputation to her conduct before her marriage, but insinuated that even to this day she was a "woman of the grove and brake"—for centuries the Welsh term of opprobrium for the loosest female characters.

Squire Griffiths easily tracked Owen to Ty Glas; and without any aim but the gratification of his furious anger, followed him to upbraid as we have seen. But he left the cottage even more enraged against his son than he had entered it, and returned home to hear the evil suggestions of the stepmother. He had heard a slight scuffle in which he caught the tones of Robert's voice, as he passed along the hall, and an instant afterwards he saw the apparently lifeless body of his little favourite dragged along by the culprit Owen—the marks of strong passion yet visible on his face. Not loud, but bitter and deep were the evil words which the father bestowed on the son; and as Owen stood proudly and sullenly silent, disdaining all exculpation of himself in the presence of one who had wrought him so much graver—so fatal an injury—Robert's mother entered the room. At sight of her natural emotion the wrath of the Squire was redoubled, and his wild suspicions that this violence of Owen's to Robert was a premeditated act appeared like the proven truth through the mists of rage. He summoned domestics as if to guard his own and his wife's life from the attempts of his son; and the servants stood wondering around—now gazing at Mrs. Griffiths, alternately scolding and sobbing, while she tried to restore the lad from his really bruised and half-unconscious state; now at the fierce and angry Squire; and now at the sad and silent Owen. And he—he was hardly aware of their looks of wonder and terror; his father's words fell on a deadened ear; for before his eyes there rose a pale dead babe, and in that lady's violent sounds of grief he heard the wailing of a more sad, more hopeless mother. For by this time the lad Robert had opened his eyes, and though evidently suffering a good deal from the effects of Owen's blows, was fully conscious of all that was passing around him.

Had Owen been left to his own nature, his heart would have worked itself to doubly love the boy whom he had injured; but he was stubborn from injustice, and hardened by suffering. He refused to vindicate himself; he made no effort to resist the imprisonment the Squire had decreed, until a surgeon's opinion of the real extent of Robert's injuries was made known. It was not until the door was locked and barred, as if upon some wild and furious beast, that the recollection of poor Nest, without his comforting presence, came into his mind. Oh! thought he, how she would be wearying, pining for his tender sympathy; if, indeed, she had recovered the shock of mind sufficiently to be sensible of consolation! What would she think of his absence? Could she imagine he believed his father's words, and had left her, in this her sore trouble and bereavement? The thought madened him, and he looked around for some mode of escape.

He had been confined in a small unfurnished room on the first floor, wainscoted, and carved all round, with a massy door, calculated to resist the attempts of a dozen strong men, even had he afterward been able to escape from the house unseen, unheard. The window was placed (as is common in old Welsh houses) over the fire-place; with branching chimneys on either hand, forming a sort of projection on the outside. By this outlet his escape was easy, even had he been less determined and desperate than he was. And when he had descended, with a little care, a little winding, he might elude all observation and pursue his original intention of going to Ty Glas.

The storm had abated, and watery sunbeams were gilding the bay, as Owen descended from the window, and, stealing along in the broad afternoon shadows, made his way to the little plateau of green turf in the garden at the top of a steep precipitous rock, down the abrupt face of which he had often dropped, by means of a well-secured rope, into the small sailing-boat (his father's present, alas! in days gone by) which lay moored in the deep sea-water below. He had always kept his boat there, because it was the nearest available spot to the house; but before he could reach the place—unless, indeed, he crossed a broad sun-lighted piece of ground in full view of the windows on that side of the house, and without the shadow of a single sheltering tree or shrub—he had to skirt round a rude semicircle of underwood, which would have been considered as a shrubbery had any one taken pains with it. Step by step he stealthily moved along—hearing voices now, again seeing his father and stepmother in no distant walk, the Squire evidently caressing and consoling his wife, who seemed to be urging some point with great vehemence, again forced to crouch down to avoid being seen by the cook, returning from the rude kitchen-garden with a handful of herbs. This was the way the doomed heir of Bodowen left his ancestral house for ever, and hoped to leave behind him his doom. At length he reached the plateau—he breathed more freely. He stooped to discover the hidden coil of rope, kept safe and dry in a hole under a great round flat piece of rock: his head was bent down; he did not see his father approach, nor did he hear his footstep for the rush of blood to his head in the stooping effort of lifting the stone; the Squire had grappled with him before he rose up again, before he fully knew whose hands detained him, now, when his liberty of person and action seemed secure. He made a vigorous struggle to free himself;

he wrestled with his father for a moment—he pushed him hard, and drove him on to the great displaced stone, all unsteady in its balance.

Down went the Squire, down into the deep waters below—down after him went Owen, half consciously, half unconsciously, partly compelled by the sudden cessation of any opposing body, partly from a vehement irrepressible impulse to rescue his father. But he had instinctively chosen a safer place in the deep seawater pool than that into which his push had sent his father. The Squire had hit his head with much violence against the side of the boat, in his fall; it is, indeed, doubtful whether he was not killed before ever he sank into the sea. But Owen knew nothing save that the awful doom seemed even now present. He plunged down, he dived below the water in search of the body which had none of the elasticity of life to buoy it up; he saw his father in those depths, he clutched at him, he brought him up and cast him, a dead weight, into the boat, and exhausted by the effort, he had begun himself to sink again before he instinctively strove to rise and climb into the rocking boat. There lay his father, with a deep dent in the side of his head where the skull had been fractured by his fall; his face blackened by the arrested course of the blood. Owen felt his pulse, his heart—all was still. He called him by his name.

"Father, father!" he cried, "come back! come back! You never knew how I loved you! how I could love you still—if—Oh God!"

And the thought of his little child rose before him. "Yes, father," he cried afresh, "you never knew how he fell—how he died! Oh, if I had but had patience to tell you! If you would but have borne with me and listened! And now it is over! Oh father! father!"

Whether she had heard this wild wailing voice, or whether it was only that she missed her husband and wanted him for some little every-day question, or, as was perhaps more likely, she had discovered Owen's escape, and come to inform her husband of it, I do not know, but on the rock, right above his head, as it seemed, Owen heard his stepmother calling her husband.

He was silent, and softly pushed the boat right under the rock till the sides grated against the stones, and the overhanging branches concealed him and it from all not on a level with the water. Wet as he was, he lay down by his dead father the better to conceal himself; and, somehow, the action recalled those early days of childhood—the first in the Squire's widowhood—when Owen had shared his father's bed, and used to waken him in the morning to hear one of the old Welsh legends. How long he lay thus—body chilled, and brain hard-working through the heavy pressure of a reality as terrible as a nightmare—he never knew; but at length he roused himself up to think of Nest.

Drawing out a great sail, he covered up the body of his father with it where he lay in the bottom of the boat. Then with his numbed hands he took the oars, and pulled out into the more open sea toward Criccaeth. He skirted along the coast till he found a shadowed cleft in the dark rocks; to that point he rowed, and anchored his boat close in land. Then he mounted, staggering, half longing to fall into the dark waters and be at rest—half instinctively finding out the surest foot-rests on that precipitous face of rock, till he was high up, safe landed on the turfy summit. He ran off, as if pursued, toward Penmorfa; he ran with maddened energy. Suddenly he paused, turned, ran again with the same speed, and threw himself prone on the summit, looking down into his boat with straining eyes to see if there had been any movement of life—any displacement of a fold of sail-cloth. It was all quiet deep down below, but as he gazed the shifting light gave the appearance of a slight movement. Owen ran to a lower part of the rock, stripped, plunged into the water, and swam to the boat. When there, all was still—awfully still! For a minute or two, he dared not lift up the cloth. Then reflecting that the same terror might beset him again—of leaving his father unaided while yet a spark of life lingered—he removed the shrouding cover. The eyes looked into his with a dead stare! He closed the lids and bound up the jaw. Again he looked. This time he raised himself out of the water and kissed the brow.

"It was my doom, father! It would have been better if I had died at my birth!"

Daylight was fading away. Precious daylight! He swam back, dressed, and set off afresh for Penmorfa. When he opened the door of Ty Glas, Ellis Pritchard looked at him reproachfully, from his seat in the darkly-shadowed chimney-corner.

"You're come at last," said he. "One of our kind (i.e., station) would not have left his wife to mourn by herself over her dead child; nor would one of our kind have let his father kill his own true son. I've a good mind to take her from you for ever."

"I did not tell him," cried Nest, looking piteously at her husband; "he made me tell him part, and guessed the rest."

She was nursing her babe on her knee as if it was alive. Owen stood before Ellis Pritchard.

"Be silent," said he, quietly. "Neither words nor deeds but what are decreed can come to pass. I was set to do my work, this hundred years and more. The time waited for me, and the man waited for me. I have done what was foretold of me for generations!"

Ellis Pritchard knew the old tale of the prophecy, and believed in it in a dull, dead kind of way, but somehow never thought it would come to pass in his time. Now, however, he understood it all in a moment, though he mistook Owen's nature so much as to believe that the deed was intentionally done, out of revenge for the death of his boy; and viewing it in this light, Ellis thought it little more than a just punishment for the cause of all the wild despairing sorrow he had seen his only child suffer during the hours of this long afternoon. But he knew the law would not so regard it. Even the lax Welsh law of those days could not fail to examine into the death of a man of Squire Griffith's standing. So the acute Ellis thought how he could conceal the culprit for a time.

"Come," said he; "don't look so scared! It was your doom, not your fault;" and he laid a hand on Owen's shoulder.

"You're wet," said he, suddenly. "Where have you been? Nest, your husband is dripping, drookit wet. That's what makes him look so blue and wan."

Nest softly laid her baby in its cradle; she was half stupefied with crying, and had not understood to what Owen alluded, when he spoke of his doom being fulfilled, if indeed she had heard the words.

Her touch thawed Owen's miserable heart.

"Oh, Nest!" said he, clasping her in his arms; "do you love me still—can you love me, my own darling?"

"Why not?" asked she, her eyes filling with tears. "I only love you more than ever, for you were my poor baby's father!"

"But, Nest—Oh, tell her, Ellis! you know."

"No need, no need!" said Ellis. "She's had enough to think on. Bustle, my girl, and get out my Sunday clothes."

"I don't understand," said Nest, putting her hand up to her head. "What is to tell? and why are you so wet? God help me for a poor crazed thing, for I cannot guess at the meaning of your words and your strange looks! I only know my baby is dead!" and she burst into tears.

"Come, Nest! go and fetch him a change, quick!" and as she meekly obeyed, too languid to strive further to understand, Ellis said rapidly to Owen, in a low, hurried voice—

"Are you meaning that the Squire is dead? Speak low, lest she hear. Well, well, no need to talk about how he died. It was sudden, I see; and we must all of us die; and he'll have to be buried. It's well the night is near. And I should not wonder now if you'd like to travel for a bit; it would do Nest a power of good; and then—there's many a one goes out of his own house and never comes back again; and—I trust he's not lying in his own house—and there's a stir for a bit, and a search, and a wonder—and, by-and-by, the heir just steps in, as quiet as can be. And that's what you'll do, and bring Nest to Bodowen after all. Nay, child, better stockings nor those; find the blue woollens I bought at Llanrwst fair. Only don't lose heart. It's done now and can't be helped. It was the piece of work set you to do from the days of the Tudors, they say. And he deserved it. Look in yon cradle. So tell us where he is, and I'll take heart of grace and see what can be done for him."

But Owen sat wet and haggard, looking into the peat fire as if for visions of the past, and never heeding a word Ellis said. Nor did he move when Nest brought the armful of dry clothes.

"Come, rouse up, man!" said Ellis, growing impatient. But he neither spoke nor moved.

"What is the matter, father?" asked Nest, bewildered.

Ellis kept on watching Owen for a minute or two, till on his daughter's repetition of the question, he said—

"Ask him yourself, Nest."

"Oh, husband, what is it?" said she, kneeling down and bringing her face to a level with his.

"Don't you know?" said he, heavily. "You won't love me when you do know. And yet it was not my doing: it was my doom."

"What does he mean, father?" asked Nest, looking up; but she caught a gesture from Ellis urging her to go on questioning her husband.

"I will love you, husband, whatever has happened. Only let me know the worst."

A pause, during which Nest and Ellis hung breathless.

"My father is dead, Nest."

Nest caught her breath with a sharp gasp.

"God forgive him!" said she, thinking on her babe.

"God forgive me!" said Owen.

"You did not—" Nest stopped.

"Yes, I did. Now you know it. It was my doom. How could I help it? The devil helped me—he placed the stone so that my father fell. I jumped into the water to save him. I did, indeed, Nest. I was nearly drowned myself. But he was dead—dead—killed by the fall!"

"Then he is safe at the bottom of the sea?" said Ellis, with hungry eagerness.

"No, he is not; he lies in my boat," said Owen, shivering a little, more at the thought of his last glimpse at his father's face than from cold.

"Oh, husband, change your wet clothes!" pleaded Nest, to whom the death of the old man was simply a horror with which she had nothing to do, while her husband's discomfort was a present trouble.

While she helped him to take off the wet garments which he would never have had energy enough to remove of himself, Ellis was busy preparing food, and mixing a great tumbler of spirits and hot water. He stood over the unfortunate young man and compelled him to eat and drink, and made Nest, too, taste some mouthfuls—all the while planning in his own mind how best to conceal what had been done, and who had done it; not altogether without a certain feeling of vulgar triumph in the reflection that Nest, as she stood there, carelessly dressed, dishevelled in her grief, was in reality the mistress of Bodowen, than which Ellis Pritchard had never seen a grander house, though he believed such might exist.

By dint of a few dexterous questions he found out all he wanted to know from Owen, as he ate and drank. In fact, it was almost a relief to Owen to dilute the horror by talking about it. Before the meal was done, if meal it could be called, Ellis knew all he cared to know.

"Now, Nest, on with your cloak and haps. Pack up what needs to go with you, for both you and your husband must be half way to Liverpool by to-morrow's morn. I'll take you past Rhyl Sands in my fishing-boat, with yours in tow; and, once over the dangerous part, I'll return with my cargo of fish, and learn how much stir there is at Bodowen. Once safe hidden in Liverpool, no one will know where you are, and you may stay quiet till your time comes for returning."

"I will never come home again," said Owen, doggedly. "The place is accursed!"

"Hoot! be guided by me, man. Why, it was but an accident, after all! And we'll land at the Holy Island, at the Point of Llyn; there is an old cousin of mine, the parson, there—for the Pritchards have known better days, Squire—and we'll bury him there. It was but an accident, man. Hold up your head! You and Nest will come home yet and fill Bodowen with children, and I'll live to see it."

"Never!" said Owen. "I am the last male of my race, and the son has murdered his father!"

Nest came in laden and cloaked. Ellis was for hurrying them off. The fire was extinguished, the door was locked.

"Here, Nest, my darling, let me take your bundle while I guide you down the steps." But her husband bent his head, and spoke never a word. Nest gave her father the bundle (already loaded with such things as he himself had seen fit to take), but clasped another softly and tightly.

"No one shall help me with this," said she, in a low voice.

Her father did not understand her; her husband did, and placed his strong helping arm round her waist, and blessed her.

"We will all go together, Nest," said he. "But where?" and he looked up at the storm-tossed clouds coming up from windward.

"It is a dirty night," said Ellis, turning his head round to speak to his companions at last. "But never fear, we'll weather it?" And he made for the place where his vessel was moored. Then he stopped and thought a moment.

"Stay here!" said he, addressing his companions. "I may meet folk, and I shall, maybe, have to hear and to speak. You wait here till I come back for you." So they sat down close together in a corner of the path.

"Let me look at him, Nest!" said Owen.

She took her little dead son out from under her shawl; they looked at his waxen face long and tenderly; kissed it, and covered it up reverently and softly.

"Nest," said Owen, at last, "I feel as though my father's spirit had been near us, and as if it had bent over our poor little one. A strange chilly air met me as I stooped over him. I could fancy the spirit of our pure, blameless child guiding my father's safe over the paths of the sky to the gates of heaven, and escaping those accursed dogs of hell that were darting up from the north in pursuit of souls not five minutes since."

"Don't talk so, Owen," said Nest, curling up to him in the darkness of the copse. "Who knows what may be listening?"

The pair were silent, in a kind of nameless terror, till they heard Ellis Pritchard's loud whisper. "Where are ye? Come along, soft and steady. There were folk about even now, and the Squire is missed, and madam in a fright."

They went swiftly down to the little harbour, and embarked on board Ellis's boat. The sea heaved and rocked even there; the torn clouds went hurrying overhead in a wild tumultuous manner.

They put out into the bay; still in silence, except when some word of command was spoken by Ellis, who took the management of the vessel. They made for the rocky shore, where Owen's boat had been moored. It was not there. It had broken loose and disappeared.

Owen sat down and covered his face. This last event, so simple and natural in itself, struck on his excited and superstitious mind in an extraordinary manner. He had hoped for a certain reconciliation, so to say, by laying his father and his child both in one grave. But now it appeared to him as if there was to be no forgiveness; as if his father revolted even in death against any such peaceful union. Ellis took a practical view of the case. If the Squire's body was found drifting about in a boat known to belong to his son, it would create terrible suspicion as to the manner of his death. At one time in the evening, Ellis had thought of persuading Owen to let him bury the Squire in a sailor's grave; or, in other words, to sew him up in a spare sail, and weighting it well, sink it for ever. He had not broached the subject, from a certain fear of Owen's passionate repugnance to the plan; otherwise, if he had consented, they might have returned to Penmorfa, and passively awaited the course of events, secure of Owen's succession to Bodowen, sooner or later; or if Owen was too much overwhelmed by what had happened, Ellis would have advised him to go away for a short time, and return when the buzz and the talk was over.

Now it was different. It was absolutely necessary that they should leave the country for a time. Through those stormy waters they must plough their way that very night. Ellis had no fear—would have had no fear, at any rate, with Owen as he had been a week, a day ago; but with Owen wild, despairing, helpless, fate-pursued, what could he do?

They sailed into the tossing darkness, and were never more seen of men.

The house of Bodowen has sunk into damp, dark ruins; and a Saxon stranger holds the lands of the Griffiths.

Elizabeth Gaskell – A Short Biography

Elizabeth Gaskell (1810-1865) is today remembered as one of the greatest female writers of the English tongue. She was born in Chelsea on September 29th, 1810, to William Stevenson, a Scottish Unitarian minister before becoming the keeper of the Treasury Records, and to Elizabeth Holland. Both parents inculcated their strong Unitarian beliefs into their children, including Elizabeth who was often reluctant to display her religious convictions, though. A number of her novels were highly controversial for dealing with delicate political and social issues of the Victorian Age such as the exploitation of the working class and the situation of women in society. These included *Mary Barton: A Tale of Manchester Life*, *Ruth* and *Cranford*. Due to their concentration on the observation of the Victorian society and the mechanisms that governed social classes, Gaskell's works are today of much interest not only to literary scholars and critics, but also to social historians.

The early death of Elizabeth Gaskell's mother represented a crucial turning point in the daughter's life. Indeed, her father decided to send her to be brought up by her maternal aunt in Knutsford, Cheshire. Such a crucial development left Gaskell deprived of the care of both her parents. Her father soon remarried and had other children from his new wife. Although Gaskell spent most of her childhood in Cheshire away from her father and his new family, she used to have a positive attitude towards her half-siblings.

Gaskell's aunt encouraged her to learn the rules of language and writing and to read books. In the beginning, Gaskell attended a school at Bradford House before she went to another school in Stratford-upon-Avon in 1824 where she was able to learn about the arts, literature and Victorian traditions and manners. In addition, and despite being separated from her family, her brother John and her father used to encourage her to read and write, often providing her with necessary books and writing material. After finishing school, Gaskell paid some visits to maternal relatives in London, Newcastle upon Tyne and Edinburgh. In 1828, her brother John, who worked in the merchant navy, disappeared definitively on a journey to India. This disastrous loss depressed her father and she had to go to his household to nurse him for the next year before he died.

In 1832, Elizabeth Gaskell, née Stevenson, fell in love with William Gaskell and married him. Like Elizabeth's father, William was a Unitarian minister and was equally fond of literature and the arts. Unitarianism, which was largely present in Elizabeth Gaskell's childhood and married life, is a Christian doctrine that believes in divine unity as opposed to Trinitarianism. Unitarianism is also a highly rationalistic belief that highlights the fundamental role of the human in the world. This set of beliefs greatly marked Elizabeth Gaskell's life and work whose professional career as a published writer actually started when she settled with her husband in Manchester. The industrial aspect of the city had a great impact on Gaskell who felt the need to speak about poor workers and their exploitation by large industrial companies. A collection of poems and short stories entitled "Sketches among the Poor" first appeared in 1837 in *The Blackwood Magazine*. The work, which was co-authored by her husband, was followed by the anonymously-published "Clopton Hall" and then by "Notes on Cheshire Customs" in 1840. Both short works were included in compilations. Gaskell later published "Libbie Marsh's Three Eras" and "Sexton's Hero." However, Gaskell's first major work, which did not bear her real name either, was *Mary Barton: A Tale of Manchester Life* published in 1848.

According to biographers, the decision to write *Mary Barton* came after Gaskell lost her nine-month son named William when her husband advised her to resort to writing in order to escape depression. The novel was an immediate success and many critics still believe it to be Gaskell's masterpiece. Set in the industrial city of Manchester, the novel displays the hardships of the working class. It centers on the eponymous character whose father is concerned with the state of the poor and who gets involved in trade-unionism. Mary, who has to choose between her two suitors, chooses the wealthier, Carson, in an attempt to help her father. However, she soon that she discovers that she committed a mistake by refusing Wilson, the man that she really loves. Apart from the events centering on Mary's life, the description of the poverty of workers was shocking to many. Manchester business owners felt offended by the novel which, they believed, was unfairly harsh on them.

On the other hand, literary critics and novelists of the time rather hailed Gaskell's refined writing style. These included renowned figures like William Makepeace Thackeray, Thomas Carlyle, John Ruskin, and mainly the great Victorian novelist Charles Dickens who soon invited Gaskell to publish her stories in his periodical *Household Words*. During this period, Gaskell was also busy being a mother and a minister's wife. She was also engaged along with her husband in numerous charitable activities. With Dickens, Gaskell first published *Lizzie Leigh* in 1850 which dealt with the taboo subject of prostitution, to be followed by *The Well of Pen Morfa* and *The Heart of John Middleton*.

Generally, Gaskell was not only an excellent writer whose stories and style impressed the greatest among her fellow Victorian literary figures, but also a social critic whose works often created a lot of polemics. After the polemic caused by Mary Barton among capitalist classes, she published another novel entitled *Ruth* in 1853 to cause much more uproar. *Ruth*'s plot follows the life of a young female who engages in a sensual relation and gives birth to an illegitimate child. The novel unveils Victorian social hypocrisy and focuses on the miserable state of women in society. The ensuing scandal might have caused embarrassment even to her husband as a copy of the book was burnt in his same church. Most critics of the book who declared the anathema missed the story's moral lesson and caused the book to be banned from libraries.

Four years later, another polemic rose after the publication of Gaskell's biography of her close friend Charlotte Bronte. It was right after the death of Bronte in 1855 that her father Patrick Bronte asked Gaskell to do the work and she accepted. *The Life of Charlotte Bronte* caused a great controversy and this was because many of the people portrayed in the work complained about being misrepresented. Some even threatened to sue Gaskell and the latter was forced to publish an apology in *The Times* and to make some revision and modifications for the final version. In the meantime, Gaskell continued publishing her stories in Dickens's *Household Words* and later in his *All the Year Round* as other important novels of hers were gaining popularity such as *Cranford* (1853) and *North and South* (1854).

Many of Gaskell's short stories are today believed to have a great influence on the Gothic genre which witnessed a revival after her death with writers like Sheridan Le Fanu, Robert Louis Stevenson and Bram Stoker. Towards her twilight years, Elizabeth Gaskell started sending her stories to *The Cornhill Magazine* which was edited by another outstanding Victorian literary figure, William Makepeace Thackeray. Soon Gaskell started the serialization of the "saddest story [she] ever wrote," *Sylvia's Lovers* (1863). The story is set back in the late eighteenth-century at the time of the Napoleonic wars. It follows the character of young Sylvia Robson, her simple family life and her secret romantic relation with Charlie Kinraid. In 1864, Gaskell published her four-part novella *Cousin Phillis* which is considered by many critics as a crucial achievement. They also agree that the novella unintentionally fits as a prelude for Gaskell's final remarkable achievement *Wives and Daughters*.

Wives and Daughters (1864-1866) is Elizabeth Gaskell's last novel first serialized in *The Cornhill Magazine* and of which the last installment was completed posthumously by Frederick Greenwood. Nonetheless, the book is considered by many as Gaskell's finest achievement and masterpiece. It tells the story of Molly Gibson who is raised by her widowed father. As a middle-class woman, she knows that she is not suitable for the son of a gentry family, the Hamleys, with whom she falls in love. Her father marries again and Molly is far from appreciating her too ambitious stepmother who also wishes to match her own daughter to one of the Hamleys. By and large, the novel is a social investigation and a condemnation of social hypocrisy. It shows Gaskell's characterization skills at their best.

Elizabeth Gaskell's interest in social criticism is one of the most important features of her fiction. It made some critics compare her to Friedrich Engels and even to Carl Marx. Her novels are today used not only as literary references, but also as historical and sociological sources for researchers interested in the Victorian society. On November 12th, 1865, Elizabeth Gaskell died in Holybourne, Hampshire, after suffering from a heart attack a month earlier. A memorial dedicated to the Victorian novelist is located in The Poets' Corner in Westminster Abbey next to Britain's greatest writers and poets.

Elizabeth Gaskell – A Concise Bibliography

Novels
Mary Barton (1848)
Cranford (1851–53)
Ruth (1853)
North and South (1854–55)
Sylvia's Lovers (1863)
Wives and Daughters: An Everyday Story (1865)

Novellas and Collections
The Moorland Cottage (1850)
Mr. Harrison's Confessions (1851)
The Old Nurse's Story (1852)
Lizzie Leigh (1855)
My Lady Ludlow (1859)
Round the Sofa (1859)
Lois the Witch (1861)
A Dark Night's Work (1863)
Cousin Phillis (1864)

Short Stories
Libbie Marsh's Three Eras (1847)
The Sexton's Hero (1847)
Christmas Storms and Sunshine (1848)
Hand and Heart (1849)
The Well of Pen-Morfa (1850)
The Heart of John Middleton (1850)
Disappearances (1851)
Bessy's Troubles at Home (1852)
The Old Nurse's Story (1852)
Cumberland Sheep-Shearers (1853)
Morton Hall (1853)
Traits and Stories of the Huguenots (1853)
My French Master (1853)
The Squire's Story (1853)
Half a Life-time Ago (1855)
Company Manners (1854)
The Poor Clare (1856)
The Doom of the Griffiths (1858)
Right at Last (1858)
"The Manchester Marriage" (1858)[19]

The Haunted House (1859)[20]
The Crooked Branch (1859)
The Half-brothers (1859)
Curious If True (1860)
The Grey Woman (1861)
The Cage at Cranford (1863)
Crowley Castle (1863)

Non Fiction
Sketches Among the Poor (poems 1837)
An Accursed Race (1855)
The Life of Charlotte Brontë (1857)
French Life (1864)